A TALE OF

Two War Wives

Meenu Mann

authorHOUSE®

AuthorHouse™
1663 Liberty Drive
Bloomington, IN 47403
www.authorhouse.com
Phone: 1-800-839-8640

Published by AuthorHouse 7/26/2013

ISBN: 978-1-4918-0217-5 (sc)
ISBN: 978-1-4918-0215-1 (e)

Library of Congress Control Number: 2013913231

Table of Contents

1975—London

CHARLIE

*T*he scene at the airport was typical—families saying good-bye to their loved ones, businessmen shaking hands with their prospective clients, tourists grimacing at the sound of pneumatic drilling (the airport's attempt to extend its boundaries and give it a modern look) as they posed for their souvenir photographs with Scotsmen in kilts. The flight to London was chockablock. The cricket World Cup was drawing a lot of attention. More than a dozen countries were to participate in this event at Lord's Cricket Ground, which was good news for the local economy. The traffic on the trains and buses created so much chaos that the upper-middle class, TV crews, and sports teams chose to travel by air.

Numerous fragrances from the duty-free shops and aromas from the food café filled the air, along with the grinding noises from the wheels of luggage pulled by passengers. Clearly visible at this modern, sophisticated airport was the massive investment in tourism—one could buy nearly anything, from electronics to fine bottles of wine to books to neckties to caviar and all sorts of souvenirs from the airport boutiques. Charlie's stomach rumbled for the taste of a warm cinnamon roll with a cup of tea, but first he needed to use the lavatory. The waft of strong cleaners hit him as he stood in the queue. His nose twitched, and he sneezed loudly, spraying the guy in a suede jacket in front of him. Charlie apologized profusely, even though the man didn't pay any attention.

Charlie's request for an upgrade was politely declined by a poised and tactful air stewardess, who remained calm under the duress. Boarding the plane was smooth. He shoved his duffel bag—with tad bit of difficulty—in the compartment above his seat and sat next to young man who appeared to be barely in his early twenties. He looked as if he might be preparing for a job interview with his self-absorbed look and Filofax planner in his lap. Charlie took out the in-flight safety instruction card from the seat pocket and browsed through it. It was a short flight from Edinburgh to London. He had a three-hour layover at Heathrow before his next flight to New Delhi, India—his very first travel expedition. He'd never gone on any adventures in his college days. When his friends would spend school breaks visiting the south of France or a Spanish villa for fun, Charlie would head home to see his mother.

Now, as he reclined his airline seat and closed his eyes, his life ran through his mind like a movie …

Charlie was born to Annie, who was married twice,

first to Peter McPhee and then to Joe Hunter, but she kept her last name as Benson, the same as Granny Mary's. Neither of these gentlemen was Charlie's father. His teenage years in Edinburgh were happy and without any major catastrophe. It wasn't until much later, as a young adult at college, that he appreciated life at home. His good performance in academics secured his acceptance at Royal Holloway University in London for his undergraduate program. At seventeen years of age, Charlie couldn't have felt more scared. The thought of leaving home and his mother and granny was overwhelming, but he was a tough, rugged teenage boy, so he pretended to be happy and excited. His mother wanted him to move on with his life, get a higher education, and succeed in life, but Charlie somehow felt trapped in a world of terrifying solitary confinement of his own mind. College seemed like a gigantic obstacle. His mother's ambitions for him put him under a lot of pressure, but he took the challenge. His mother, Annie, was blessed with a character that combined sensitivity and wry detachment, a rare and precious mixture indeed.

Peter McPhee, Annie's first husband, was a young, handsome, and ambitious officer with the British army. He had been assigned to the post in India during the "Free India" movement in 1930. Annie had met and married him in London, when he was stationed there for a few months. Many new revolutions were erupting and causing the British Empire a concern they could have done without at the time of national crisis, as war loomed in Europe. Annie, however, fell head over heels in love with Peter and saw no sense in anything else but marrying him and later following him to India.

Annie was always sure of what she wanted to do. Her resilient determination is what Charlie admired most about her. If one mentioned the most decisive people on earth, his mother would be on top of the list. She encouraged Charlie and guided him through school. Her desire for him to choose English literature as his major worked well for him. She could have easily been a fine teacher, given a chance. She had a marvelous talent of connecting and analyzing people, yet she lived her life simply. Her adventurous spirit and amazing sense of exploration got her through life without distress, considering her choices in life. From a very young age, she learned to disguise her feelings of love, hate, anger, fear, and hope. Her preference of living life on her own terms raised a few eyebrows, but she chose to devote her time to meaningful relationships only. Annie was generous at heart and very sensitive to others' needs, sometimes more than her own.

Charlie couldn't remember his mother ever giving him a warm hug or a kiss on a cheek, yet he knew that she loved him more than anything in the world. Her way of expressing love was different from most other mothers. She never overreacted when Charlie got hurt by falling off his bike or over other silly stuff kids did. She would just pat him and whisper in his ear, "If you are smart, you won't do that again." Her simple statement housed itself in Charlie's brain. If he ever did something wrong and got in trouble, she never reprimanded him or scolded him, but he never repeated the same mistake again. As a single child brought up by a single mother, the two had a mutual understanding and respect for one another.

Annie was a beautiful woman, whom Charlie loved to watch for hours as a little boy—her soft white skin, short blonde wavy hair, and deep blue eyes. Her kind face was very transparent and couldn't hide her emotions, radiating when she was happy and turning somber when she was deep in thought. As a little boy, Charlie realized that he looked nothing like her and often wondered if he was an adopted child. He saw other kids who looked like their mothers or fathers, but he never questioned his mother until later in life. He called his mother "Mother Annie" as a child and continued to address her that way until he became a father himself. Then he switched to "Ma."

Bedtime stories were the most fun times of Charlie's childhood. He felt very special when his mother told him stories, such as that he came into this world as a prince from a distant land, who had magical powers.

Less fun for Charlie were trips to the barber. He hated the way the barber pulled on his hair while brushing out the tight curls. And when the barber finished trimming Charlie's hair and turned him around to see the mirror, Charlie could hardly recognize himself. Still, he would nod his thanks, even though tears glistened in his eyes and a forced smile was on his lips. Eventually, after his mother recognized the distress the barber caused Charlie, she let him wear his hair long.

1947—Scotland

ANNIE, MARY, AND CHARLIE

Annie, Mary, and Charlie lived in a tiny cottage on the north side of Edinburgh, a place called Inveresk. Annie made her living as a governess to a wealthy family's two children. The family had made their fortune from a slave-owning sugar plantation in Jamaica. Annie was offered a private accommodation on the property, but she had declined the offer. She had not mentioned Charlie or Mary in her application for employment, as she didn't think it was relevant. Charlie was ten years old, a quiet child who didn't make much fuss. His granny Mary, who was retired, stayed at home and took on knitting as a hobby, as it had become quite a popular trade during World War II. She knitted scarves and gloves for the family and looked after Charlie when he came back home from school. Granny Mary checked his schoolwork while Annie worked to provide for them. Granny Mary was an excellent teacher, most patient and systematic.

Annie allowed Charlie to be independent. He could

do whatever he wanted to do, go wherever he wanted to go, and be with whoever he wanted to be with, as long she knew what, where, and who with. He had more freedom growing up than any of his friends. He was independent, yet he was responsible enough to hold himself accountable, as he knew the consequences for unacceptable behavior. Losing his weekend treat of his favorite television shows was too harsh of a punishment for him to be disorderly. Finishing his homework assignments on time and preparing himself for the annual test and exams was his own responsibility. Annie didn't interfere or nag Charlie about his study schedule; as long as his progress report was excellent, she was laid back. Her own upbringing had been strict, formal, and slightly prim, of which she strongly disapproved, but she had to abide by the rules as a child. Still, she was careful in her own dress, manners, and demeanor, even though she didn't impose any house rules on Charlie.

It was a relief that Charlie loved school and knew the importance of education. The belief, which was drilled into his mind, that a better education promises better prospects in life was the pivotal truth of life. He had not seen anyone else in the entire village work as hard as Annie worked. She got up early to fix breakfast, packed his lunch, and then walked almost a mile to the big mansion, where she worked from eight o'clock in the morning until five o'clock in the evening. On her way back from work, she often stopped to do the grocery shopping, and once home, she would do other chores—cooking dinner, cleaning, washing, and even taking time to read books to Charlie. He admired, appreciated, and respected his mother for providing a good life. There were a lot of poor people in his neighborhood, and some kids his age went to bed without food at night. Charlie could not comprehend the thought of being hungry. He ate all the time, and Granny Mary used to complain that he ate like a horse.

Looking back, Charlie realized he had a very steady childhood. He didn't have a single bad memory. Life was good, even for a mixed-race boy. He happily adhered to all the rules at home and school. Lack of a father figure was not his mother's concern. Annie maintained a healthy lifestyle at home, and she, Mary, and Charlie played cards and board games together and worked on jigsaw puzzles and school projects.

The other boys at school talked about the amount of domestic violence and abuse that went on in their families. Drunk, frustrated men took out their anger on their wives and kids. The economic situation of the country was appalling. Poverty, which led to crimes and other social injustice, including bullying and name-calling, even in the school playgrounds, was common. Young boys followed the same pattern as their fathers and dealt with situations by being angry. One of Charlie's closest friends, Sam, often begged to come over to Charlie's house to do homework, especially if it was an important assignment. Sam could never be certain if he was going to be caught in his parents' clamors at home.

Charlie liked school, even though he had his share of bullying and teasing. He was called a "half caste," which would make him cringe. Racist and heartless adults also set out to wound him with hurtful comments. They addressed him with disgust and told their kids to stay away from him, as if he was a dirty, diseased boy. At an age when Charlie wanted to fit in, he stood out. When he reported the bullying incidents to his mother, asking her why he was different, she simply told him, "Don't be a sheep; just following and being like others is easy. Being different is good. Be yourself. You are beautiful and bright, and some people are jealous of you." Charlie didn't believe her, but that was because he didn't want to be different. It was lucky that he was a big, strong boy who could handle the physical nature of the abuse—no one challenged him physically more than once—but emotional abuse was where Annie and Mary stepped in. They addressed the parents of the abusers and the school principal, notifying them that they would not hesitate to involve the authorities if the emotional bullying did not stop.

The school principal liked Charlie a lot, and he immediately called an emergency meeting to speak to his fellow teachers, telling them to report the bullying issues in the school. Most teachers were successful in stopping the bullies by giving them warnings that their grades and passing marks would suffer tremendously if the bullying continued. Within days, bullying almost at came to a halt—the boys who picked on Charlie regularly simply left him alone.

Most evenings, as Annie cooked the meals, Granny Mary watched game shows on television like *What's My Line?* and *Good Old Days*. Charlie did his homework and later helped with the dishes and took out the garbage. He enjoyed being at home with his mother and his granny in the safe and secure environment. Both women in his life were his life coaches and character builders who shaped him into a happy, stable person. A lot of young adults didn't realize the gifts bestowed upon them, but Charlie was mature enough to recognize this gift. Granny Mary often called him her "handsome boy," and Annie would then say, "Handsome is as handsome does." It was a polite criticism wrapped up in a caution for him not to get bigheaded about his appearance.

He dragged his feet when it was time for him to go to London University, but his mother made sure he got on that bus. It wasn't that he didn't want to be away from home; it was just that it cost a lot more to go to London University than to go to the local University of Edinburgh. He didn't feel right being a financial burden for his mother, but he could not defy her insistence and authority. She assured Charlie that it would be all right, and she handed him a bankbook and other important notes, which he shoved in the pockets of his jacket. She also placed a business card in his hands that read "Douglas Jake Law Firm," attorneys she asked him to contact in London. It had to do with her trust fund and reserve fund she had put aside for Charlie's education.

And so he was ceremoniously pushed out of the nest and took lodgings with eight other university students. He soon found that living away from home as a young adult gave him a peculiar sensation, neither pleasurable nor distasteful, merely something to which he was not accustomed. It was like walking on a pond covered in ice.

1975—On Flight to India

CHARLIE

The pilot turned on the Fasten Seatbelts sign as the stewardesses, with their happy smiles, walked the aisle to make sure that all passengers were following the safety rules. Charlie felt as if they almost took it as an offense if a passenger was a little delayed in figuring out what to do. Some passengers did have genuine reasons to ignore their first request, partly because their hearing was impaired due to plugged ears, and there were others who just couldn't find the darn belt ends stuck between the seat pads in the poorly lit cabins. Charlie didn't get annoyed easily, but the passenger across the aisle from him was giving a stewardess a lot of grief. He refused to fasten his seatbelt, complaining that it didn't fit him right, challenging her authority, and calling her a "dipstick." Charlie was shocked by the man's discourteous behavior. Obviously, he was shocked that the love affair between the airlines and the passengers was fading away. The romantic and adventurous spirit of the passengers was replaced by a disappointing, bitter traveler. Charlie couldn't help but intervene. "Lay off and be courteous," Charlie told the man. "She's just trying to do her job." The man totally ignored Charlie.

The young man sitting next to Charlie looked as if he was going to puke. Charlie pointed toward the airsick bag, just in case. When the plane reached its destination and Charlie and his seatmate were walking off the plane, the man admitted to having anxiety disorder. Charlie wished him good luck and then went to one of the airport pubs while he waited for his connecting flight. It was a little too early for a beer, but there was nothing else to do at the airport. He ordered a lager and glanced over his boarding pass for the gate number for the next flight.

When his flight was called, he climbed aboard the brand new British Airways 747 waiting on tarmac in its full splendor, along with the other passengers. Once in the air, he learned that on an international flight, there were crêpes flambé at 35,000 feet, wine in wine glasses, steak dinners served on porcelain, real cutlery, and after-dinner cigars—not that he smoked, but the stewardess was happy to offer the male passengers a light. It was all a very languid and unhurried flight. Even though his trip was only for a few days, he still felt trepidation, and apprehension of the unknown had been instilled in his mind without his permission. He'd had his share of feeling unnerved in his career, but this was by far the worst of it.

Saying good-bye to his wife, Joan, and their ten-year-old daughter, Sasha, that morning still felt raw. Joan worked for a major industrial research company that aimed to develop the first speech-driven word processor. They had married right after she finished her PhD, and Sasha was born two years later. A healthy beautiful baby changed their lives. They were overjoyed and exhausted at the same time. Joan worked from home, which made it possible for Charlie to take the trip to India.

Annie had insisted it was time for Charlie to meet his father. He had always intended to relish the cultural diversity, but the thought of meeting his father for the first time was unnerving. His father's wife, Maya, had requested that Annie visit too, but Annie's health didn't allow her to travel. Her fibromyalgia was nonresponsive to the various treatments she had tried. Regardless, she had no desire to visit India again; apparently, it had brought her enough heartache.

1918—England

ANNIE

Annie was born in February 1909 to the fairly wealthy John and Maggie Clayton in Camberley, Surrey. She was their only child, and both parents doted over her. Her father was a physician and her mother a nurse who helped him run a country practice in a small village where they lived.

By the time she was six years old, Annie had become a bright little girl who loved adventures, and her parents' friends remarked on her inquisitive mind and fun-loving nature. One of her father's friends in particular, Dr. Rodney, who was a regular visitor, took keen interest in Annie.

At first, no one suspected anything, but when Annie started having trouble concentrating in school and started to avoid her parents' friends, her mother became concerned. Annie only wanted to play in her room when Dr. Rodney and his wife visited. Still, her mother would insist that Annie greet their guests, even though she screamed her head off when her mother made her leave her room. She dragged her feet, and her mother spanked her. With teary eyes, Annie would say hello to Dr. Rodney and his wife, and he would pull Annie in his lap while he showed her fatherly affection. Annie sometimes struggled to get loose and ran off to the kitchen, looking for her governess. Her parents first thought Annie's behavior was rude, and occasionally, she was punished for that.

It was months later, when her schoolteacher felt something wasn't right, that Annie's withdrawn behavior and failing schoolwork was brought to her parents' attention, who decided what was needed was tough punishment.

Dr. Rodney came to the family home often with his wife for informal dinners and tea. No one thought anything of his going to Annie's bedroom to "say good night," nor did they know of his sick need to touch her, fondle her, and hold her close to him. Annie, exhausted after a busy day, was unaware of his actions, but one night, she felt sticky fluid in her panties. Annie was worried that perhaps she had wet herself. She felt too ashamed to tell her mother.

Dr. Rodney was a well-respected man in the community and quite popular among top-class doctors and surgeons, but he leaned toward very liberal thinking. He always laughed about rules for children—he didn't believe in a firm structure for family. John and Maggie Clayton thought Dr. and Mrs. Rodney were ignorant, as they had no children of their own and so had no idea or experience in such matters. The Claytons disregarded

Dr. Rodney's opinions on childrearing, and they vetoed his suggestion that Annie call him by his first name—it was quite impossible for John and Maggie to permit their child to address her elders so casually.

Annie liked to break her parents' rules, and so she often got in trouble with her governess. The governess was a sound woman who didn't tolerate any nonsense. She took pride in being strict and formal with her charge. She herself was very prim and proper in her dress and manners. Annie liked to do things her own way; she was headstrong and could not be convinced to wear or eat something if she didn't feel like it. Her governess, who believed in strict discipline, would force Annie to obey. Mrs. Clayton, who spent much of her day with her husband in the office, didn't care how the governess handled the situation as long as it was handled before she got home. She didn't like confrontation.

It was the summer of 1918 when Dr. Rodney and his wife offered to share their summer house on the river with the Claytons. In past years, Annie's family would go to Runnymede, a small town on the banks of River Thames, for picnics and boat rides. The Claytons would hire a boat, and Annie's father would fish, her mum would read magazines, and Annie would play on the boat until it got dark. Annie loved summer, when all the trees and shrubs were a lush green, and the water, so crystal clear and inviting, rose to the edge of the riverbank. Lots of wealthy people were out with their boats and fishing rods.

Then Dr. Rodney spoiled Annie's summer plans by cleverly enticing her parents to join him and his wife at the summer house. Annie's desire to be on the boat was so urgent that she ignored the wickedness of Dr. Rodney and accompanied her parents. The Claytons graciously accepted, almost pitying the childless couple for their loneliness. That first weekend, Dr. Rodney sexually abused Annie in his home. She was nine years old.

Poor Annie was traumatized by her ordeal, and in extreme shock and shame, she felt as if her soul had walked out the door, and there was nothing left but her dirty body. She sat there, full of self-contempt, for few minutes before she gathered her courage and walked straight to her father. She reported the abuse and begged to leave Dr. Rodney's place at once. Her father didn't know how to react to such absurd news—he knew Annie loved to make up stories, but this bizarre and despicable talk from her pushed him past his limit. He barked at his wife to deal with her.

Annie was terribly distressed that her mother's first reaction was denial that anything had happened. Instead, she was ordered to go to bed. Later, however, Mrs. Clayton started showing severe psychological symptoms of being a victim herself. She felt deep shame and guilt for neglecting her daughter.

The trauma left Annie feeling that no one would believe her. *When I am bad, people send me away*, she thought. *Big people hurt me. I am a bad person. No one loves me, and no one is there for me. I'll have to take care of myself.*

After sounds of scuffling in her parents' room, muffled cries, and arguments, the Claytons left the Rodneys' summer house to go home. A few weeks later, Annie was shipped to a boarding school in London, miles away from home. That was the last summer she spent with her parents. Now that her schooling was away from home, she was forced to spend summers on school premises, or she visited with other kids' families. She only came home for short visits at the Christmas holidays. Her parents never brought up the subject of Dr. Rodney. Annie never found out what happened to Dr. Rodney, but she was pleased that she never saw him again.

Annie's parents died in a car accident shortly after her thirteenth birthday. She didn't know why, but she cried for her mother. It was ironic that as she was grieving for her parents, she needed them to comfort her. She wondered if they died because of her. She asked herself questions, such as "Will I die like them too? Who will look after me now?" She felt helpless and bereft. She was left with plenty of money in her trust fund but no one to love her.

After her parents' death, Annie's behavior toward adults changed. She didn't feel protected anymore. She was damaged goods. Who would want her? At school, she showed a brave face to teachers and school mates, but at night, when she was alone, she cried.

Her English teacher, Ms. Mary Benson, was the only adult with whom Annie felt comfortable enough to let her guard down. Perhaps it was Ms. Benson's red curly hair or her freckles or her Cockney accent from the East End, but something about her made Annie feel comfortable and not nervous. Ms. Benson was different from all the others; she was approachable. Annie followed her in the corridors in between her classes, trying to get her attention, asking if she could borrow her books or making small conversation as a way to reach out to her.

Annie practiced the conversation in her head and prepared herself for all the relevant questions and answers. Soon, they broke the barrier of the teacher/ student relationship and became secret friends. Annie's sudden change in behavior—she seemed less distracted and more attentive in class—was obvious to other teachers and students. Ms. Benson had opened a dialogue with Annie in such a way that she not only felt calmer but also became interested in school lessons. The damage caused by criticism and neglect had caused Annie to lose self-confidence, but Ms. Benson's attention gave Annie's self-esteem a huge boost.

Mary Benson realized that Annie was a bright but troubled child, and she wanted Annie to learn to apply her energy in a constructive way. Annie was clearly not interested in PE, so Mary Benson stimulated her to try her aptitudes for expression in a drama class. They both were thrilled when they had a chance to go on a school trip to see the London Science Museum. As one of the chaperones on the bus, Ms. Benson was careful not to give other pupils any reason to suspect that Annie was her favorite. But on the drive back, Annie shared the seat with Ms. Benson, which cheered Annie up immensely. Her admiration and infatuation with her teacher was such that she imitated her Cockney accent, and she secretly wished her hair was brunette instead of blonde. Annie purposely didn't brush her hair after washing it, hoping it would get curly. Most days, she looked like a total mess, and it was one of those particular days when the school photographer was taking pictures that Annie was called to the nurse's office, where Ms. Benson made Annie brush her hair. She even braided it for her, telling her how pretty she looked.

It was months later in their friendship that Annie mentioned Dr. Rodney to Ms. Benson, who maneuvered the conversation very delicately without probing too much. She comforted Annie and tried to help her understand that it wasn't her fault. Although Annie had come a long way, she couldn't bring herself to forgive and forget her parents' emotional abuse and neglect. She wished her parents had believed her and not sent her away to a boarding school. She remembered her mother crying bitterly, but she was too weak to oppose her husband. She wondered about all the mothers; did they all follow their husbands and neglect their children? She wanted to believe that her mother was the best mother in the world and that she loved and cared for Annie. It wasn't until much later that Annie understood that her mother kept silent, probably because of financial insecurity or moral obligation to her husband. She had simply obeyed her husband's decision with regard to their only daughter. The thought almost numbed Annie.

Annie's display of sexual knowledge and behavior beyond what was appropriate for her age was shocking to other students and teachers. Annie was acting out; she felt isolated and frightened. She didn't like other girls her age, who were curious about her and regarded her as different. Some pitied her, and some were overly friendly. Sometimes she felt violated and shunned. She retaliated in the only way she knew how—embarrassing others with her quick wit and confronting teachers, staff, and other students and putting them on the spot.

Annie became the school bully, yet someone to whom the girls went with their troubles. Even older girls asked advice and valued her opinion. Her defiant nature got her in trouble, but she never wavered when someone weaker needed her help.

Annie was relentless and ignored any reprimands about her behavior. She'd inherited her parents' large estate, and the school board needed her funds to keep the school running.

Annie soon learned that she could break any rule and get away with it. Even in the strict environment of the convent school, Annie went her own way. She couldn't be a captive of the dorms; her love for the outdoors and being out in the snow and rain exhilarated her. She was street-smart and had developed a strong defense mechanism. She had learned the chilling fact, in the offices of attorneys, that the world she lived in couldn't care less for anyone's emotional needs. It was strictly business in most parts, and she was a piece of furniture that could be placed anywhere, as long as the school board got its funds, trustees and attorneys got paid their fees, and whoever benefitted in whatever form. Even social workers and distant relatives turned a blind eye to her needs—and that didn't go unnoticed in Annie's eyes. No one offered to take Annie under their wing, and that hurt Annie the most. She wanted to be accepted as a child, to have a home like other kids, to have grandparents and siblings … but she knew it was just a dream.

Annie's trustee and attorney were approached by the school board concerning Annie's disruptive behavior. They'd had enough complaints to expel Annie, but it was in the school's best interest to keep her on its register. Half of the students had already left due to the sickly economy. The Great War had done plenty of damage, causing young families to lose their fathers and their income. Lots of families were displaced due to the war.

Ms. Benson was aware of Annie's tendency toward intense preoccupation. She recognized Annie's vulnerability and victimization, and that frightened her. She felt that in such a mental state, Annie required extensive supervision and therapeutic help. She took the initiative and spoke to the principal about it. The school nurse suggested a professional evaluation. They took Ms. Benson's advice and arranged for Annie to see a child physiatrist in London—Ms. Benson's deceased husband's friend and colleague, who specialized in children's mental diseases. An appointment with Dr. Johnson was set up for the following week.

The school nurse was to accompany Annie for her first evaluation. Annie, however, was not informed of these arrangements until the principal called her into the office on the day of her appointment. Upon hearing this, Annie froze and refused to go. Ms. Benson was called in to escort Annie to her appointment with Dr. Henry Johnson.

Dr. Johnson was renowned in his field, having done extensive research on the subject and having written a couple of books on human behavior. To Annie's relief, he turned out to be very nice—a kind, friendly figure who handled Annie professionally. Annie didn't realize how naive and vulnerable she'd been in thinking that she could hide all her pain. After numerous sessions with Dr. Henry Johnson, however, Annie still wasn't willing to talk about her abuse with her peers—she remained aloof and detached from the other pupils. She felt no one needed to know, as none of them could do anything about it—her own parents hadn't done a damn thing about it.

Finally, after months of consistent effort with Dr. Johnson and Ms. Benson, a new Annie emerged. With careful consideration and immense persuasion, social services allowed Ms. Benson to become Annie's foster mother. Annie and Ms. Benson both were overjoyed with the decision. Ms. Benson had been praying for this day with all her heart. Saving Annie was her life's mission at that point. Legalities were examined and evaluated, and three weeks later, Annie moved in with Ms. Benson. Annie's life did a complete about-face. Each found companionship in the other. It was what Annie wanted most—a protector, a mother figure, someone to whom Annie could talk and have all to herself. Ms. Benson performed the duties of a teacher well at school, but she performed even better as a mother to Annie at home.

Annie could not bring herself to address Ms. Benson as Mum. She wished her to be, but it was not easy. Ms. Benson told Annie she could call her by her first name at home, if she wanted to. From then on, Annie called Ms. Benson "Mother Mary."

Sharing a home with Mary Benson felt a little weird in the beginning. She still had memories of her father, who always ruled the house. Mary was a female living alone, but she gave Annie a safer haven, where she developed a sense of security. Mary shared many of her life experiences with young Annie, hoping Annie would learn that when bad things happen in life, one's motto should be, "Make the most of it." Annie's grades started improving at school and so did her self-confidence. Annie felt wholesome again.

Annie expressed interest in attending the college for higher education, rather than taking a job she was offered at the local attorney's office as a typist. Mary was thrilled, even though she knew it would cost a substantial fee. She encouraged Annie to meet new people and even correspond with pen pals abroad. They took weekend trips to London museums and art galleries and visited the East End regularly. Annie screamed in excitement, laughed as loudly as she could, but she was never reprimanded for such behavior.

Mary often checked on Annie at the attorney's office where she worked on Saturdays as a part-time typist. Seeing her at her desk, humming a tune with pencil in her mouth brought a smile to Mary's lips. She saw her young self in Annie. Annie acted responsibly toward her school lessons and her weekend job at the attorneys, and her interaction with other girls and teachers at school improved tremendously. Annie was preparing for the entrance exams for formal education on the day Mary received a letter from her sister, Sally, who had moved to Scotland right after her marriage to a war photographer. It was rare that Mary received any correspondence from her family members. Most of her aunts and uncles lived in London or nearby, but everyone had drifted apart. Mary and Sally were just a year apart in age and very similar in temperament, and both had minds of their own. Mary had always looked up to her older sister, who did fairly well, so she was delighted that Sally had written to her.

1920s

MARY AND SALLY

*M*ary and Sally grew up in a London pub, which was run and later owned by their father, Jack Benson, and his wife, Lucy. The original owner had made his fortune by letting others ruin theirs by drinking in his pub. Local women often were up in arms when their husbands spent their paychecks at his pub. Mary and Sally's father was one of the regular pub-goers who enjoyed a drink or two after a hard day's work.

Jack was smart and ambitious man who saw an opportunity to run a better business. His keen and observant nature earned him a chance to prove himself. He offered to run the place as a manager and turn it around. Soon the 'Coach and Horses Pub' became popular among the locals. After the death of the pub owner few years later, Jack and Lucy took over and ran the place as their own.

Jack, being a shrewd pub owner and competitive businessman made few enemies in his business. Lucy was a beautiful redhead who made sumptuous meals in the pub's kitchen. Her steak and kidney pies became so popular that top-notch businessmen and people from out of town came to check it out. In 1899, Sally met Ernie McPhee, a photographer of London's bridges, which he sold to magazines. They married that same year and had a son, Peter, the following year. During the Great War, Ernie became a famous war photographer.

Mary and Sally grew up in an environment where they were mostly surrounded by half-drunk men, cursing and behaving badly, and sometimes well-dressed and respectable men also showed up with their lady friends. As they grew up, neither sister had any interest in similar kind of lifestyle. Sally married her Scotsman and moved away. Mary was courted by many men, but she didn't love any of them—not until she met a fine gentleman in her father's pub who came in for drinks with two other couples. James, who happened to be a nobleman, found Mary very attractive. Yet her unapproachable personality as she took drink orders and ignored the men who were eyeing her made him wonder about her. She didn't seem to care when a man paid her compliments. James was amazed that Mary didn't look twice at him. Handsome and wealthy, he was known as a most desirable and eligible bachelor.

Several weeks later after James' first visit to the pub, he came back to ask the landlord about the redheaded girl who had waited on him. Jack eyed James and informed him that his daughter Mary was the redhead and that she was a teacher at the school. "She only works in the pub to help me out from time to time," he said.

James introduced himself to Jack and asked his permission to court his daughter. Jack agreed, and after a brief courtship, the couple married in 1906. They had a blissful life together for several years—and then James was called for duty to his country and was killed in 1914. Mary was heartbroken, but decided the only way to deal with her heartache was to continue teaching at the boarding school. And that's where Annie entered in her life. Her need to care for a daughter and have a family was finally accomplished.

Sally's letter to Mary announced that her son, Peter, was in London for few weeks. Mary had mixed feelings of joy and woe, as she had not seen her nephew in all these years. She was eager to see her grown-up nephew—a handsome military officer by the look of the pictures she had seen at her parents' home few weeks ago.

1928

PETER McPHEE

*P*eter McPhee, born to Sally and Ernie McPhee in 1900, was born and raised in Edinburgh. As a little boy, Peter was shy, meek, and very clingy. Sally begged Mary to visit her when Peter was a boy, but Mary never had an opportunity. In Peter's teenage years, he grew confident, outgoing, and popular. During the uprising and violent acts of revolution in 1928 in India, Peter was drafted and packed to go to London for training. The majority of the officers like Peter were trained at Sandhurst Military Academy. These cadets, who achieved the highest level of training, were destined for the Indian army in India.

Mary and Annie read the newspaper each morning, and they observed a lot of news about the "Quit India" movements in the far land. The general essence of the news was that British reigned over India with force, and Indians had started rebelling. Times were little crazy, and emotions were high, as according to the latest Rowlett Act, the British government could imprison anyone without a trial or a conviction. There were widespread protests to this law. Mary felt very angry and bitter, remembering the Jallianwala Bagh massacre almost ten years earlier, when British troops marched to Jallianwala Bagh (a public garden) in the northern Indian city of Amritsar, accompanied by an armored vehicles with machine guns mounted on top. There, General Dyer ordered his men to open fire on a peaceful gathering of men, women, and children. Since there was no other exit but the one already manned by the troops, people desperately tried to exit the park by climbing over the walls and were immediately shot down. Hundreds of innocent men, women and children jumped into a well to escape the bullets. The incident was reported in all major newspapers as a purely evil act. More than a thousand people were massacred, and the event was condemned worldwide. The general public in England were stunned by the cruelty. General Dyer, however, was admired and praised for his ruthlessness, even though he massacred innocent people.

News of a similar uprising in India occurred when the British government increased the tax on the land. When the poor Indians were not able to pay the high taxes, their lands were confiscated. Mahatma Gandhi was creating problems for British with his nonviolent methods of revolution. He urged the farmers not to pay the tax, declaring the hike unjust. Finally, the government agreed to hold an inquiry into the justification of the tax hike, and they returned all confiscated land and items to the farmers. News in the paper of Gandhi's campaigns was quite amusing, especially the one when he took to spinning the charkha (spinning wheel) and boycotted foreign goods and clothes. He urged the general public and was successful in convincing them to burn their foreign possessions on public bonfires. There was a lot of unrest, however, and British people's opinions were split.

Peter was liberal minded, yet very disciplined and structured, as he should have been as a young military officer. He was kind at heart but felt weak and helpless in certain situations, such as when he was ordered to report at the scene where Bhagat Singh, an Indian revolutionary, threw a bomb in the Central Legislative Assembly to protest against the passage of the Public Safety Bill. The aim was not to kill, for the bombs were relatively harmless, but to make a statement. Peter had picked up some leaflets from the rubble that read, "If the deaf are to hear, the sound has to be very loud." The objective of the chaos was to get arrested and to use the trial court as a forum for propaganda, so that people would become familiar with the movement and ideology. Peter could not but admire the guy.

Peter was housed at the army barracks nearby but wanted to pay his respects to his only aunt. Mary arranged to meet him at the Coach and Horses. He was exactly as Mary had imagined—tall and handsome, just like his dad. He was very pleasant to talk to and had a very impressive personality. Peter updated Mary on his career and where he was headed.

Mary immediately thought of Annie—she was nine years younger than Peter, but Annie looked a lot more mature than girls her age. Perhaps it was her fashionable dress style or her confident outlook on life. Annie was a beautiful, healthy, young lady with an aura around her that people noticed when she walked in a room. Mary reflected on her relationship with James, who also had been nine years older than she was.

"Peter, I'd like you to come to the house for tea at the weekend," Mary offered sweetly. She hoped to introduce him to Annie, but first she wanted to discover if he had someone special in his life. "Bring a friend, if you like,"

"Thank you, Aunt Mary," Peter answered. "I'd be pleased to come for tea, but I'll come alone."

Annie was getting ready to leave for her shift at the pub when Peter arrived. "Do sit down, Peter," Mary said, offering tea and biscuits but glancing over her shoulder to watch for Annie. A few minutes later, Annie came down wearing a light pink blouse and a long gray pencil skirt with ankle boots. Her short, wavy blonde hair framed her pretty face and made her look like a movie star. People complimented Annie on her appearance all the time, but Annie just remained humble. She didn't have to make much effort. She believed in good hygiene, a healthy diet, and a good posture. Annie's fashion sense was at its peak, as the preferred look was the dropped waistline, longer skirts, and a straight tunic bodice, a silhouette with a boyish look that totally eliminated womanly curves. In broader shoulders, shorter hair, and narrow hips, Annie looked very beautiful. Her piercing blue eyes, pearly white teeth, and statuesque figure took Peter's breath away. He had never seen anyone so beautiful. Good-looking gals like her were rarely available; they were either taken up by the theater companies or taken by rich, noble husbands.

"It's a pleasure to meet you, Annie," Peter said, extending his hand when Mary introduced him. Annie thought Peter was quite handsome and charming, and she fumbled for words as she shook his hand and smiled. Their mutual attraction was clear.

"I'm ... I'm sorry, but I ... I have to go," Annie stammered. "I'm afraid I'll be late for work." She dashed out of the living room, leaving Peter to call out after her, "It was lovely to meet you," but Annie didn't reply.

After she'd gone, Peter sighed and said to Mary, "Mum never mentioned you had a daughter."

Mary smiled knowingly. "Annie is my foster daughter," she said, giving him all the information he needed.

After that, Peter visited the house every weekend, hoping to see Annie. Most often, though, Annie was busy working her part-time job as a typist. Annie's trust fund would not be available to her until she reached the age of twenty-five, so she wanted to save money for her college expenses. She was seriously planning to go to London University and majoring in English literature the following spring. Still, she managed to be around when Peter visited, and their mutual interest in each other soon meant that they couldn't see enough of each other. Mary Benson was happy to see this relationship develop. Annie seemed very happy, and Peter was a perfect gentleman.

Annie wasn't familiar with the military lifestyle or its protocol. She was surprised to learn that Peter was required to travel abroad and might be away for several months. Mary had known better; she had been through a similar experience years ago. Annie developed a fear of losing Peter, and her dreams of going to the university went out of the window. She decided to put her college education on a back burner. Her immediate need was to stay with Peter at all costs.

Peter had similar feelings for Annie, and so he proposed to her late one afternoon as they sat on a bench by the riverbank. When he dropped to his knee to pop the question, passersby cheered him on. Annie blushed and hid her flushed cheeks with her hands, but she said yes without hesitation. They kissed as the evening sun dropped into River Thames. The beautiful sunset, birds flying above their heads and boat horns blasting away in distance were the perfect signs for a happy union. God's most precious gift for Peter and Annie was the sudden shower of rain, and they both got drenched, locked in each other's arms, kissing passionately.

Mary was in the kitchen making tea when Annie barged in through the kitchen door, soaked from the rain. "Guess what?" she exclaimed excitedly. Mary opened her mouth to scold Annie for dripping on the kitchen floor, but before she could say anything, Annie continued, "Peter proposed today, and I said yes!"

Mary, who was holding a hot pot of tea, quickly put it back on the stove and gave Annie a kiss on her cheek. "I'm so happy for you, Annie," she said sincerely. "Peter's a wonderful man. My blessings are always with you—you know that." She hugged Annie and shooed her from the kitchen, saying, "Now get into a hot bath before you catch a cold. I'll have tea ready when you're finished."

Once Annie was warm and dry and had changed into her night clothes, the idea of a hot cup of tea was replaced with a glass of sherry, and they sat in front of the fire, celebrating the good news. "You know," Mary admitted, "I set up Peter's initial visit in the hope that the magic might work."

Annie laughed, tipping her glass of sherry to Mary. "I'm so glad you did!"

Although Mary was pleased for Annie, she was apprehensive about Annie's choosing to get married right away instead of going to college. Mary genuinely cared for and loved Annie, and she wanted to make sure that Annie had a skill, a trade, or education so she could stand on her own feet to support herself in hard times. No matter how much fortune there was in Annie's trust fund, she would need a constant source of money to survive a long life.

Mary called her sister, Sally, the next morning, and both were equally excited for the wedding. Sally and Ernie made plans to attend the wedding, and Mary helped Annie choose her wedding dress. They decided it was going to be a simple ceremony at the church, followed by drinks and supper at the pub. Peter and Ernie took the responsibility of finding the right pub. Both decided on the King's Arms, a traditional local pub tucked away on a quiet back street.

Annie had numerous twists and turns in her life, but falling in love with Peter felt so perfect and so right. He had accepted her for who she was, without changing her to who he wanted her to be. All the loneliness that had afflicted her in her young life had escaped her now. Love was like a magician that pulled Peter out of the hat for Annie. Sometimes she wondered if it was real, and she pinched herself as she questioned if she deserved to be so happy and why she was scared. Before she could find answers to her own questions, she was swept away with emotions. She firmly told herself to grab all the joy of life when it presented itself and to appreciate life's simple pleasures.

1929

PETER AND ANNIE'S WEDDING

*I*n the spring of 1929, Peter and Annie got married in the presence of Peter's parents, Mary, and the couple for whom Annie worked at the law firm. After the ceremony at the church, they headed to the pub for drinks and supper. The King's Arms was bursting with regular customers—the public bar was packed, and the saloon bar at the rear was set up for their family dinner. People cheered wildly and greeted the newlywed couple when they saw Annie enter in her bridal gown. Many men started singing and patting Peter on the back as the wedding party made their way through the public area. The King's Arms was charming with its bare floorboards, heavy curtains, old paintings on the walls, and lamps on the windowsills. Ernie felt proud and happy for his son, as the pub landlord led them to the private dining room with a brick floor and sky-lit roof. The room was nicely decorated and had a cozy feel to it. Sally and Mary enjoyed reminiscing about the old days at the pub. Ernie called out to the landlord "Drinks on me!" More cheers followed.

Later that night, the newlyweds were off on their honeymoon in Cornwall, the beautiful southwestern peninsula of England, bounded by the Atlantic Ocean and the English Channel. This longest stretch of continuous coastline happened to be one of the sunniest areas in the UK. Peter's travel agent had highly recommended this popular destination for honeymooners. Annie's employers had packed a picnic hamper with couple of bottles of champagne, a fine cheese selection, and pork pies for the journey. The attorney for whom Annie worked had lent them his spare car for a week, and his wife had presented them with pearl earrings for Annie and cuff links for Peter. Mary offered her contribution by paying for the small cottage Peter and Annie had rented for a week in Cornwall. Peter's parents took care of the pub bill. The couple was extremely grateful for their generous gifts. Peter's only friend, Mike Owens, a naval officer and Peter's roommate could not attend the wedding, but he had promised to meet up with them at the pub and later offered to drive them to the bed-and-breakfast that Peter had booked for their wedding night. Mike's girlfriend worked there and had suggested the place; she got them a great deal on their honeymoon suite.

The clerk at the reception desk welcomed and congratulated them as they checked in for the night. The young bellhop carried their luggage to their room and gave them extra attention, thinking they were wealthy. Peter saw him eyeing Annie and shooed him away with nice tip. The window in their third-floor room offered a view of rows of dimly lit houses and streetlights reflected on wet, shiny black roads. It looked like modern art drawn on the canvas. Peter closed the window as the chilled air on his face tickled him.

The room was fairly large but cozy, with lots of frilly pillows, heavy curtains with valences, and carved mahogany furniture. It made them feel very grand. Next to the bed was a tray with a complimentary bottle of champagne and two glasses. Fresh flowers in a crystal vase were beautifully displayed on a side table, next to which was a note that Peter had slipped there without Annie's noticing. Now, she spied the envelope and tore it open to read. It read: "If I don't romance you, I don't deserve you. If I don't adore you, I don't deserve you. If I don't cherish you, I don't deserve you. In you, I have found the greatest joy of my life. Be mine!"

Annie's dream of a romantic husband came true as she lunged toward Peter for a kiss. Her black-and-white life had transformed into a colorful one. She'd dreamed of having a loving husband, but until she'd met Peter, she'd assumed that sweet romance and chivalry only existed in romantic novels and movies. Now, Peter cupped Annie's face in his hands and kissed her passionately. Suddenly, Annie drew back from him and went to use the bathroom, saying she needed to freshen up. Peter was taken aback a bit. She was gone a long time, and Peter finally knocked on the door to see if she was all right.

Annie emerged from the bathroom and apologized as Peter poured champagne in the glasses. "I have no idea what came over me," she said feebly. She didn't want to share her demons with her husband on their wedding night, but the physical part of the marriage seemed a tough prospect. Peter knew that Annie had not had any previous relationships, so he said gently, "I know that the first time can be the scariest experience for a girl. It's okay if you aren't ready for action. We don't have to do it until you are ready."

Annie relaxed a bit. They drank champagne, slipped into their night clothes, and talked about everything—except sex. Annie allowed Peter to hold her against him and massage her neck and shoulders until she fell asleep. Peter, who had a full-on erection in the process, had to go out on the adjoining balcony to smoke a cigarette.

It was not until early morning, when Annie was slowly waking from her dreams, that Peter was inside her. Annie was so relaxed—half asleep, half intoxicated with champagne—that she responded beautifully to the lovemaking. They both reached orgasm at the same instant and went back to sleep. When they finally awoke, they realized they had missed their breakfast and were starving. They didn't want to miss their dinner reservation at the restaurant in Cornwall, where they were headed for their honeymoon. They had jam croissants and tea in the room, quickly changed into fresh clothes, and headed downstairs, where their car was waiting for them. The receptionist handed them the car keys and a picnic hamper, and they took off.

They experienced the most picturesque landscape as they passed through the gorgeous countryside. The long drive on the A39 contained sharp, hairpin turns, which gave Annie thrills as Peter drove with the windows down. As they were passing through a little village, they pulled up along the side of the road to get out and stretch their legs. They hadn't talked much in the car, but there was a newfound bond between them. "Let's have our picnic over there," Peter said, pointing to an open field with trees and a small creek." He got the picnic basket from the car, and Annie followed him along the trail with a blanket. She spread the blanket on the grass under a tree and then opened the picnic hamper and poured lemonade from a flask. Peter watched his wife with puppy eyes and kissed her on her mouth. Annie kissed him back, but she was hungry now, and she wasn't going to let him fool around in the middle of an open field. She gently pushed him away and served him a sandwich and coleslaw. They ate a leisurely lunch as they relaxed on the blanket in the fresh air. Annie wished they could stay there for little longer after the lunch, for she couldn't get over the beautiful countryside, but Peter packed up the picnic basket and blanket so fast that he was in the car with the engine running when Annie joined him. Peter looked at Annie with sensuous eyes; he wanted her there and then. He reclined her front seat, made her comfortable, slipped her panties off in one quick motion, dropped his trousers, and was inside her before she could resist.

They reached the cottage by late afternoon, took a bath, and headed to the restaurant for the dinner reservation. The entire week went by much too fast. They wished they could have extended their honeymoon, but Peter was expected back at the London barracks, and Annie had to go back to work at the office. Another imminent worry nagged at their heads—finding the ideal accommodation. Annie's boss at the law firm had promised to look in to renting the third floor flat at a cheap rate.

By the time they'd been married a couple of months, they were happily living at the tiny rental flat above the law firm, where Annie worked full time now. Peter was on administrative duty, and he mostly was stationed in and around London, so he was able to come home every night. They spent their weekends together, reading newspapers in bed or going for long walks. Older ladies eagerly gave advice to newly married Annie, guiding her through the marital journey, with suggestions on how to keep the husband happy and how to cook and clean. Cooking and cleaning was not Annie's forte, but a curt warning from the ladies that "nothing destroys the happy marriage like a lazy, sloppy wife" got her attention. She organized her entire flat, from her wardrobe to kitchen pantry, and learned a couple of recipes from Mary to impress Peter. Peter was quite happy with the ploughman's cheese and pickle sandwiches that Annie usually made, and he appreciated the effort.

Christmas was just around the corner, and Annie bought a pair of leather gloves for Peter. Annie was a good conversationalist, so Peter took on the role of good listener. He laughed hard at Annie's stories, as she got carried away with them on occasion. Sometimes they sat on the bench by the riverbank and watched the ducks and geese creating a ruckus, trying to grab the pieces of bread that Annie carried in her bag. It was astonishing how quickly they gobbled them up and were hungry for more. She and Peter loved the dazzling reflection of the sun on the water, the sloshing sound of the water hitting the riverbank, and boats that were tied to the pier, rocking gently from side to side and making the rhythmic sounds. The therapeutic sounds of birds cooing and the rustling of the leaves in the trees gave Annie a comforting sensation. They walked along, hand in hand, listening to the squishing sound their feet made on sandy path.

It was the day before Peter's birthday that he was called to headquarters and presented with transfer orders to Delhi, India. It was an urgent order from the royal commanding officer. Peter was to prepare for his transfer within a fortnight. He'd been chosen to serve in the peace-time army in India. His unit's first function was primarily to organize training and get properly equipped for conventional military operations against an imperial expedition. The second function was frontier warfare and then internal security duties. Peter would be deployed to India as an officer at a captain's rank in the Royal Regiment of Artillery. He was considered a very capable and highly motivated officer who was trained for special operations. His training specialty was finding the enemy using unmanned aerial systems, radar, and by being on the front line with the infantry. His other assets were his knowledge of operating the Royal Artillery's guns, grenades, and tanks. His main job was to provide the communication and logistic support to enable the Royal Artillery to function.

Peter knew that in the past, requests for "family stay" rarely had been granted; in fact, soldiers had been discouraged from marrying. The regiment had felt that having the family in tow would cost more money and slow the movement. Peter and others felt lucky that now the army allowed officers to marry and permitted wives to accompany their husbands to far posts in India. The assumption was that the wives would behave in a maternal way to the husbands' colleagues, performing duties for them, such as laundry and basic medical care, much in the same way that army women had done—except the wives' role was unpaid. If husband was killed, it was expected that the widow would quickly take a new husband from within the group of men.

Peter and many of his senior officers who were being deployed to India were made to understand their duties and expectations. The expectations of the married women and their roles was also a well-discussed topic among soldiers. With death rates high, it was not uncommon for a man to secretly court a friend's wife, in order that he might be chosen, should her existing husband be killed in the next battle.

The British army had become more professional. The hierarchy had felt that family life should be the integral part of a soldier's life, especially abroad. Marriage was emphasized for officers in order to make them feel happy and protective of their fellow soldiers and their families. Senior officers liked the idea of having the junior officers' wives there for company and support. Women's clubs were formed all over the army camps. The bridge clubs, which were originally invented for the real need of a bridge between Indian officers and English to know one another better, became popular again. Peter was granted his request and was permitted to have his wife join him in India. His only worry was how to break the news to Annie. Against his better judgment, he announced the news that evening as they were having a couple of beers at the local pub. He assumed Annie remembered the important conversation they'd had about his career, right after they'd become serious about one another; he was mistaken.

The thought of living abroad was scary for Annie, but the thought of living without Peter terrified her. She gathered all her courage and with a big smile assured Peter that she would be fine. Couple of tears forced their way down her cheeks, but she held the rest. Peter felt guilty and angry with the situation, but Annie calmed him down. Peter was to leave right after Christmas, and Annie's plans were to join him in another six months. They promised to write to each other every week. Annie was to continue to work, and Peter would save every bit of his salary for their little place on his return.

1930—India

ANNIE FOLLOWS PETER

Annie said good-bye to Peter on a chilly morning in January 1930. Peter got in a cab with a heavy heart, and he and Annie kept waving to each other until they could not see each other any longer. As soon as Peter's cab was out of sight, Annie burst into tears. She went back to bed and cried herself to sleep.

Mary was as supportive as she could be, comforting Annie and looking out for her. She enjoyed spending time with Annie on the weekends, realizing how she'd missed her walks with Annie. Peter wrote letters every week as he'd promised, updating her on his whereabouts, his adventures in the new country, the adjustment to a different way of life, and what he referred to as the "totally crazy climate and culture." Reading Peter's letters, Annie tried to imagine the hot, humid weather and the monsoons; the trees and flowers; the birds and their chirping; and the homes and people of that faraway land. Her imagination ran wild as she envisioned Peter with the turban, wearing a white linen suit and sitting on a camel like a desert prince. She imagined herself as an Indian princess, dressed in fine jewels and gold. These were the images pasted in her mind from childhood storybooks about India.

In those long weeks after Peter left, Annie started losing interest in her daily chores and even her job. She didn't care to dress up anymore or go out with friends after work. Her lifestyle felt extremely boring and tiresome, and so she engaged in solitary hobbies like reading books and painting. She stocked up on books from the library, particularly educational books on Indian culture and history. She was intrigued by the hundreds of different languages the people spoke, by the spicy food called curry that apparently everyone ate, and the drape-like fashion called a sari that women wore. She was fascinated by the illustrated pictures in the books of the strange world of snake charmers, rickshaws, and folk dancers. She was drawn toward this new culture; it excited her and broadened her knowledge.

Britain had ruled India for over two centuries and had built a very close relationship with it. In that "golden age," during the collaborative "Raj," or British rule, the racial hierarchies and boundaries were unimportant. English men participated with locals and lived closely with them; some even had a family with local women, although that was phased out by the coercive Raj, when native women were replaced by English women. The family dynamics—interracial sexual relationships—endangered the "whiteness" of the English, and as British rulers became morally conscious, they recognized the need to uphold their racial and religious superiority.

Peter had to make all the travel plans for Annie once he got to India. He was contemplating air travel, but it wasn't a straightforward route. Imperial Airways had begun their first flight service from Britain to Karachi, India, but the route was partly covered by air and partly by trains and boats through Europe and the Middle East. Italy did not allow British aircraft to enter Italy from France, and flying over the Alps was not considered practical. The London-to-Karachi journey time was seven days, and the single fare was 130 pounds. The other option was by sea, which took up to four months. Ultimately, Peter opted for sea travel, because that would give Annie the companionship of other officers' wives and children on the long voyage.

Annie was thrilled with the news that Peter had made arrangements. She rushed to the post office the next day to complete the necessary formalities for travel documents and then informed her employers in the law office and at the pub. She had so much planning to do for this trip. She had never been away and had never been on a ship, voyaging to a dream country so far away. She praised Peter for being thoughtful that she would have the company of other families on the boat. She had no fears of any kind, except she was petrified of being sick on her travels.

Peter had informed her of the necessary list of things she was to carry at all times. She didn't even own a pair of shades or a summer hat. A little sum of money she had saved up for rainy season came in handy to splurge on clothes and other bare necessities for her trip.

It was difficult for her to decide what to take with her; she packed some of her old summer dresses, blouses, and skirts. Then she concentrated on more important things, such as getting her vaccinations, as suggested by her doctor. She packed all essential medicine in a little plastic box, along with important contact names, telephone numbers, and addresses. Peter's superiors based in London were helpful and sent messages ahead of time to their base in Delhi. Arrangements had been made for a designated driver to pick her up from the train station in Karachi and to drive her to the army base in Lahore. She was to stay in Peter's quarters and would need to follow all the rules and regulations of the base. Strict instructions were given not to engage with local Indians, for her own safety. It was quite overwhelming for Annie, but she stayed positive and did not let any frightening stories shock her. Her instinct told her that she was safe, and with her personal wall of protection was in place, Annie felt calm and safe in her own mind.

Mary was excited for Annie in her upcoming journey, and they spent a lot of time talking about India. They had discussed the type of bullying and manipulative methods Britain was using against Indian natives in their own home, but they could never express it to anyone except each other. It was such a taboo topic that schoolteachers and college professors had to swear not to indulge in political debates with their pupils; they were not to influence anyone with their knowledge on Indian politics. Annie and Mary strongly believed in fair and high moral values and condemned the British government's rule over underdeveloped nations like India. It was clear that the British ran India for the benefit of Britain, not for the benefit of India. Abuse of power over innocent people with cruelty made common British people question their government.

On the day Annie left for India, Mary dropped Annie off at the London train station with her luggage. She was catching a train to Southampton, where she would meet other families. Annie carried her hat and handbag and waved to Mary from the train window. After spending numerous hours at the library, researching India, she felt certain she had jotted down all the important information in her journals. She also carried a small notebook in which she written down certain Indian words and their meaning. Mostly, though, she relied on her mental notes. Annie was up-to-date on all the political aspects between the two countries, having read every single news column about India. She knew tension was building in the general population and that there was a general dislike of the English by Indians. Annie was very discreet and kept her opinions about national issues to herself.

In May 1930, Annie finally reached at her destination after a four-month voyage on the large steamship containing army regiments and families. Several troopships and cargo ships carrying goods and soldiers were on the same route—England–Egypt–India. It took another couple of days from Bombay to Delhi. Her ordeal during the journey was over but settling down in the new country needed lot more adjustment. The climate was much hotter than Annie had expected. Afraid of dehydration, she boiled the water daily and cooled it down for her use. Their allotted bungalow was very comfortable, with cool, glazed cemented floors partly covered by woven cotton rugs, called dhurries; ceiling fans; whitewashed walls; and a small garden. A huge bathroom with the hole in the ground as a toilet made Annie laugh—it had a water tank above the commode with the cantilever chain for flushing. A large sunken section in the corner, where a couple of buckets of water were placed, was the area for the shower. A small rectangle mirror hung above the porcelain sink. It looked very primitive, but soon Annie got used to it all. She had a team of servants to cook and clean for her. Peter's orderly, Mohan, was always present if Annie needed anything. The British had engrained the idea of an army orderly into the Indian army. It was meant to be an assistant to the officer in non-soldier duties but had become someone who was more of a personal servant for menial jobs around the house like taking the dogs for a run, looking after the personal needs of the wife and children, cleaning the car, and buying vegetables.

Annie had to quickly adapt to the requirements of her new society, and the requirements were strict. The Anglo-Indian community was insular and conformist in a very comfortable nest of habits and rules. With all the stress of moving to a new country and a new community halfway around the world, it was a relief to the newly arrived Annie that she was not expected to know it all. Peter's colleagues' wives took Annie under their wings and introduced her to the rest of the group. Annie was shocked when she asked one of the women if she knew any of the local women. The woman had replied, "Oh no! Thank goodness! I know nothing at all about them, nor do I wish to. Really, I think the less one sees and knows about them, the better."

The cultural image of British memsahibs, for which the wives of the British officials were known, disturbed Annie the most. Tyrannical and abusive, these memsahibs seemed to have little else to do but complain about the weather and gossip viciously about the locals, to whom they were intolerant and vindictive. Usually bored to death, these memsahibs also were prone to extra-marital affairs. Most memsahibs preferred to speak broken Hindi to order the servants than to trust the English-speaking servants in their homes.

Annie didn't want to be part of the rotten culture. Memsahibs had their own insecurities, evidently not only feeling threatened by the local women but also feeling the need to degrade them. At the homes of some of Peter's colleagues, Annie noticed that the wives' prejudices led their husbands to ban Indian women from their homes. British men who had Indian wives or who openly consorted with Indian women were given the cold shoulder, and anyone not abiding by the society rules was barred from men's clubs and social functions.

Stereotypical British husbands also insisted on privacy, using seclusion as an excuse to separate their wives from Indian men—their argument was that until an Indian gentleman allowed them to meet his wife; they would not allow him to meet an English lady. Annie was disgusted but she did not voice her opinions—not just yet. It was always in the evening with Peter that she discussed these issues. Both Peter and Annie thought it was a shame that the officers' wives—women who were well educated, well traveled, and came from good families—had a thorough knowledge of how to comport themselves within European society but had a lamentable ignorance of anything outside it.

Annie wanted to know more about the culture and got to know the wives of the servants. She was amazed by the efficacy with which these women worked in the kitchen, all while looking after the kids. Annie became friends with Mohan's wife, Sita, who was a pleasant girl and very eager to learn to speak English. She finished her morning chores while her baby slept in the hammock in the shade of a tree. She cooked her husband's meals on their earthen stove on an open fire. Annie watched as Sita fed her husband and baby before she helped her herself to the leftovers from her husband's plate; it gave Annie an alarming notion of selfless love.

Annie was astounded by Sita's patience and her attitude toward the rejection and abuse she received from other memsahibs. Annie saw that Sita had real strength, and her calmness and acceptance of her fate clearly made her content and happier. Annie asked Sita to join her every day for afternoon lemonade. Sita looked forward for that hour, when she dressed her baby in clean clothes and brought her along for her time with Annie. Annie loved to hold the baby in her arms and sing nursery rhymes. She learned to make rag dolls with the group of ladies who met on weekly basis for craft lessons at the club. It was later, when the others found out that Annie was breaking the rules by allowing Sita in her home and making rag dolls for her baby, that they cut Annie off from their group.

Annie, who was totally bored and repelled by these women, didn't care and continued with her friendship with Sita. They grew the vegetable garden together and tended the lemons and other fruit trees—lychees and mangoes were plentiful enough for both families. Annie taught Sita how to make English tea, and Sita taught Annie how to make mango pickle. Sita learned to write her name by practicing in the dirt. Both women learned things from each other, but Sita could not learn to call Annie by her first name—she always called her Memsahib. Annie learned enough of the local language to communicate with Sita and Mohan in their native tongue.

Peter was assigned to the Indian army under Royal Corps of Artillery, which was a separate organization to the British army, although there was a close relationship between the two. The officers in the Indian army were all British, with the exception of Indian soldiers, who performed a role within regiments similar to senior noncommissioned officers. Peter came across an Indian soldier who was with 9th Jat Regiment in the Punjab Regiment. His name was Suraj, and he was a brave, loyal servant of British Raj. An intelligent young man who was trained and managed well by the English, he had previously shown his talents and capabilities. Both Peter and Suraj joined in social and sports activities and charmed everyone around them. Suraj paid close attention to the

English gentleman's etiquette and chivalry and in time, he became familiar with the English way of life. Being handsome and popular helped him win everyone's heart, but he still had to win their trust. He rarely went home to his village in Punjab to see his family, even during his time off. Instead, he stayed at the headquarters in an effort to better himself. He was never introduced to any of the English wives.

1908 to 1918—India

BELAN IN THE ARMY;
SHANTI'S STRUGGLES

Suraj's father, Belan, at the age of thirty-three, was the first sepoy from their village to be enlisted in an Indian army. (Sepoy was the term used to indicate a native of India who was employed as a soldier by the British.) He served with the 10th Jat Battalion under the Punjab Regiment during the opening stages of the Great War; he served with his battalion on the North-West Frontier of India, taking part in active operations. In 1914, when war broke out, he was one of many brave soldiers in the regular forces in India who fought all over Asia to save the British Empire from being overrun by the Germans.

During the British Raj, when they took over the government of India, the whole military organization was rearranged. Any man could join the army as a soldier, as long as he passed certain physical tests and was willing to enlist for a number of years. Soldiers had to be of certain height and between the ages of eighteen and thirty-eight.

Thousands of men were inspired to enlist every month by the drum-beating news. There was a lot of pressure to conform, but many joined up for all sorts of reasons, including a desire to quit humdrum or grueling farm work or wanting a chance to see another country or escape family troubles.

What motivated Belan and others like him to join, however, and to fight in a war thousands of miles away from home, for a cause that did not seem to be their own, was regular income. Belan, as an Indian infantryman, earned a modest eleven rupees a month. This additional income was useful to his hard-pressed peasant family. He had traveled considerable distance to visit a recruiting office for a particular unit. With sheer hard work, dedication, bravery, and loyalty, Belan reached the rank of Subedar Major by the time he retired. After the Great War, with many idle Indian soldiers, the British Empire let go of many battalions.

During Belan's time away on duty, many incidents occurred for which he had to come home. Right after he left for training, he received a telegram from his wife, Shanti, telling him that his father had died. Shanti didn't mention the incident that had caused his death.

Later, Belan learned that his brother Tejan's teenage sons, Mangal and Shankar, had bullied his own young sons, Puran and Suraj, on their way home from school. The older cousins had been waiting in the shade of a tree by a well and had called to the younger boys. Puran walked toward his cousins, but his younger brother, Suraj, tugged on his sleeve, urging him to head home. Mangal and Shankar didn't like the younger cousins defying them, so they encircled them, blocking them from getting away. Suraj distracted the older boys and ran toward home, but the boys viciously knocked Puran down, beat him, dragged him to the well, and flung him into it. His body fell, hitting the walls of the well, and landed in the cold water many feet below. Puran used all his body strength to swim and flapped about to get hold of something.

By this time, Suraj had reached home and told his mother what the cousins had done. Shanti ran for the well with her servants and other villagers. By then, some passersby had stopped to drink water at the well and heard sounds of sobs coming from the well. They looked in to find a young boy, barely hanging to a root of the tree inside the well. They immediately reached for him with a rope and a bucket and pulled him out. Shanti got there just in time to wrap her little boy in her arms. Puran was traumatized by this horrific action; the frightened and hysterical child wanted his father by his side. Helpless and worn out, Shanti tried to console her son. She lived in a joint family home with Belan's parents and his brother Tejan and his family. She felt abandoned by her husband, who had left her and her kids in the care of his old parents and an older brother who was mean, greedy, and untrustworthy.

Her father-in-law was an old frail man on his deathbed. Shanti was a wise, quiet, and obedient woman who respected her in-laws. Shanti's being an efficient housekeeper and a compassionate human being who worked hard around the house and took good care of the children had won her mother-in-law's heart. Shanti made every effort to get along with Tejan's wife so that they could all live in harmony. Tejan and his wife resented Shanti and demanded that she work harder at home because her husband was not at home to lend a hand with the farming—they conveniently forgot the money he sent home regularly.

After the incident at the well, Shanti didn't have the courage to confront her brother-in-law, knowing he would never accept his sons' wrongdoings. She was really frightened to live under the same roof as her husband's brother. Her mother-in-law was enraged to hear of her grandson's ordeal. She confronted her son Tejan and cursed and shamed him for not disciplining his boys. As expected, Tejan wouldn't hear of it, and his sons denied it all.

The old man suffered a stroke during the commotion and passed away in the night. When Belan was informed of his father's death, he was given a leave of absence to go home for the funeral. When he reached his village, he heard about his nephews' actions against his son, and he questioned his wife and mother after the funeral rituals. Belan was furious that his brother and his nephews showed no sign of remorse. He confronted Tejan and demanded an explanation. Tejan simply avoided the subject and took advantage of the situation. Tejan offered to split the land in two equal parts and live separately. Cunning Tejan knew this would cause the family great grief, as Belan was away in the army and his sons were too young to farm. Shocked at his bold suggestion, a disappointed

Belan turned on his brother. He had expected an apology from his brother on behalf of his sons, but instead, Tejan had insulted him and his mother by demanding to split his father's inheritance. The sight of his son drowning in the well floated in front of Belan's eyes, and he couldn't control his rage. He attacked Tejan full force with his bare hands. Tejan never expected his brother to even speak up to him, let alone be violent. He felt humiliated by Belan's attacking him. Their mother was ashamed that her sons had come to blows, but she still admired Belan for also thrashing his nephews to teach them a lesson.

The mother announced her warning to Tejan in front of the entire village—that if any harm came to Belan's family, she would break all ties with him. All the villagers and the Panchayat members (a group of respected members of community who act as judges and resolve disputes) were present at the time.

Circumstances left the brothers no choice but to split the land and live separately. The land was divided in two equal parts. Village elders and the Panchayat believed it was the right of an older brother to stay in family home with the mother. But since the mother refused to stay with Tejan after that incident, it was decided that Belan should be given an extra field, with the servants lodge added to his property. Even though the main house on the farm would have been a more comfortable place for their grieving mother, she declined her comforts and embraced her daughter-in-law and son Belan. Both women declared that they would "rather live in a shack than share a home with the devil."

At the time of their eviction from the family home, Belan had felt terrible for his mother that she had to both grieve and suffer in the new surroundings. She had spent all her life in the big house with her husband. She had not had time to think things over. Perhaps she had made a harsh and hasty decision, but his mother and his wife assured him that they would be fine. Shanti collected whatever dowry her parents had given her, which mainly consisted of two bed cots, her gold jewelry, and other household and kitchen utensils. Both women realized that that they would have to be strong and vigilant on the long road ahead of them in Belan's absence. With the limited time allotted to Belan's leave of absence, the family faced a big dilemma. Belan asked for extended leave to sort out his family matters. The shameful act of Tejan and his sons had turned Belan's life upside down. He learned something new about himself, though—that not only he had showed courage in standing up to his brother, but he had relieved his mother and wife of life with the wretched man.

Belan had been taught from childhood to look up to his elders, but the notion of big brothers protecting the younger ones, and younger ones respecting older brothers had proved that lesson untrue. His brother had abused the power and trust Belan had placed in his hands while he was away. Tejan had not appreciated the help and support his wife and mother were providing to his family.

The old servants' lodge, where his family was now to live, was not safe or livable, as it had been used most recently to store agricultural tools and hay. Belan hired workers to fix the roof and the floor. The two carpenters worked day and night to repair and paint the windows and doors. Extra laborers whitewashed the inside and outside walls. Belan cleared the surrounding fields to make room for a vegetable garden and for the kids to play. Belan's priority, though, was installing a high brick wall around the house for privacy for the family. A wrought-iron gate was installed with a padlock on it.

All the villagers were extra helpful, and women in the village were kind enough to help with the cleaning and setting up the kitchen and sleeping arrangements. Men busied themselves with clearing away the surrounding fields in an effort to keep family safe from wild things. Trees were planted all around the house. New pathways were constructed for horse carts. There was much work to be done.

Tejan had shut the door in his brother's face, and Belan vowed never to set foot in his house again. There was no chance that they could go back to the house to retrieve their own things, so Belan borrowed tools from the villagers. It took an entire month to put the place together, and that was all the time Belan was allotted. Everyone's collective hard work paid off, and the place became quite comfortable to live in.

Some village elders had suggested that Belan should retire and come home, but his mother and wife supported him in his decision to stay in army for his complete enlisted time. His plan to lease his fertile land to other farmers turned out to be a better option. Lot of soldiers in the army were in the same situation. They too couldn't be there to lend a hand but had leased their land and were making good income from it. Belan didn't want his mother and wife to worry about planting and harvesting every season. His idea was to earn enough money for his family's needs while he was away, protecting the borders from the enemy. He took legal advice from reliable sources in town and made an official deal with a decent farmer, who was eager to start his life in the village. Belan was the first landlord ever to lease his land to another farmer in his village. Farmers usually didn't lease their land—their lack of education and trust in people was the biggest hurdle. Belan's time away from the village, traveling and meeting different people, had taught him to trust and have faith in people, as long as he protected himself with legalities. There were lot of parties interested in the deal, but Belan had given his word, and he honored it.

Belan's main worry was his children, especially his sons. Clearly, they were the target of their uncle's cruelty and evil scheme of eliminating them so he could absorb their share of land. Belan approached his unit's senior officer when he returned to duty, who helped him find boarding schools for his boys after he heard of the shocking treatment they'd received at home. Arrangements were made, and boys were shipped to a military school in Lahore, about fifty miles away from their village. The school was mainly for army officers' children so that their education did not suffer when their families moved from post to post. Boarding schools gave the students a stability they needed to finish their education.

Under special circumstances, Belan's superiors and

school board had made it possible for his family to send his two boys to the prestigious school with minimal school fees. Shanti and her mother-in-law visited the boys regularly but discreetly. There was not a soul who knew the whereabouts of the boys.

Puran, the elder boy in the family, was shy and physically weak, and he was very much attached to his mother. The younger son, Suraj, was bright and confident and excelled in sports and academics. Belan had encouraged both of his sons to go into military. The harsh truth was that living at home had proved to be more dangerous for the boys than sending them to the front line in the war. At least in real war, they could identify their enemies and were prepared for them.

Puran's chances for selection into the military were slim—his reluctance was quite obvious. Initially, he wanted to please his father, but he knew he wasn't cut out to be a soldier. Finally, he expressed his feelings, and Belan respected his son's wishes to come back home after matriculation and help his family run the farm. But Suraj wanted to pursue a career in the army.

The school board awarded Suraj a scholarship for further studies, which he gladly accepted. In the military academy, he could pursue his military training as well as further his education. After a long selection process, which included filling out application forms and physical exams, Suraj was accepted by the selection committee.

Puran started getting really anxious in the days following his return home from school. School routine and its curriculum had institutionalized Puran in a way that he missed it in the beginning, just like he missed home when he was first sent to school. He missed his school routine, and he missed the friends he'd made there. He missed Suraj terribly too. They had not spent a day apart since childhood. Suraj's selection into the military academy was a blow for Puran and the beginning of his lowered self-esteem and confidence. He felt he was being compared to Suraj, and villagers took his homecoming as a failure. His bruised ego later turned him into a jealous and insecure man.

Shanti and her mother-in-law had learned to manage the household and land business well in Belan's absence. They both dealt with the tenants and farm workers in a businesslike manner. Shanti kept a low profile and minded her own business. Shanti's mother-in-law was a strong, stern lady who controlled the reins of household expenses, making sure that her son's hard-earned salary didn't go to waste.

Shanti sent her daughters off to village school for their primary education, but the rest she took care of at home. Her daughters were fine young ladies who learned everything from household chores to money-managing skills from their mother and grandmother. And later, Belan, with the consent of Shanti, married his young daughters to fine young army officers who belonged to similarly respectable families.

In 1918, Belan took early retirement at the age of forty-three and returned to his village. He missed his family and wanted to take care of them. They had been left alone for far too many years. So much had gone on in his absence. Shanti had shown real strength of character in the last five years, living alone with children and her old mother-in-law, visiting the boys at the boarding schools, marrying off their daughters, and taking care of the land.

There was a grand welcome for Belan upon his return. Every one wished him well and praised him for his bravery. His mother and his son Puran, now a grown young man of eighteen, were among the crowd. Unfortunately, Puran had become a target of his uncle's threats again.

Belan and Tejan became rivals after they inherited their father's land. They shared the boundaries of their land, but their residences were quite far from each other. Brotherly rivalry was common, but some went too far. There were quite a few incidents where two blood brothers had shed each other's blood over piece of land. These two had also become enemies in later years. As Belan prospered in wealth and fortune, Tejan's empire took a downward turn. Belan was married to Shanti, a fine lady who ran the household efficiently, while Tejan's wife spent her time and energy on gossip and other useless chores. Belan believed in good education, whereas Tejan's views were of different nature. He considered himself as a landlord, and his sons were to follow him being a landlord. His sons, Mangal and Shankar, did initial schooling at their village school, but they didn't finish the matriculation.

Belan, now called Major Sahib, brought a breath of fresh air to his village. With his experience in the army, he brought discipline, organizational skills, and new ideas.

Perhaps that was the key to his success at farming. His ability to be a good listener and a communicator made him approachable and available to poor workers who were being abused and manipulated by rich farmers. He showed kindness to the weak and never judged or looked down on people. He respected his servants and taught them how to use the machines and tools. To become a role model, he taught others to take better care of the farm animals. His message to the youth was to take care of the elderly, respect the women, and love the children. Youth responded well because Belan listened to their problems and acknowledged them. He helped them with their farms and careers in the army, as they valued his experience and guidance.

Because of his kind and caring nature, everyone gave their best performance. Servants didn't whine or complain because their landlord, Belan, worked harder than they did in the fields. He was always the first one to wake up, and his disciplined and carefully planned way of work paid off. His crops did better than anyone else's. He bought tools and other heavy equipment to dig wells and made several changes in the way they practiced agriculture.

Belan kept himself in good physical shape; he exercised his weight-lifting hobby every day. He ate good food, restrained from drinking cheap homemade liquor, unlike his brother and many other landlords, who had developed a taste for this menacing hobby in their free time.

Belan popularity soon ignited more friction between him and his brother. Tejan drank until the early hours of the morning. Some nights he didn't go home and was seen loitering around the whorehouses in the early light of the morning. Those unpleasant actions led to a rift between him and his wife, who became very resentful. She refused to perform her wifely duties. Over period of time, his wife left him to join an ashram, a place of religious retreat. He was left with his children and no one to take care of them. The oldest girl was of marriageable age. The wild boys were already spoiled and obnoxious. They mistreated animals, disrespected their sisters, and refused to go to school. Seeing the trouble that Tejan was in, Belan pitied him and sent his mother over to take care of the household. With his mother's persistent efforts, Tejan agreed to marry his daughters off. Belan helped with the dowry, and his wife planned the weddings with the help of other ladies in the village. Mangal and Shankar had turned into cruel young men who took pleasure in being mean and nasty. They called their grandmother terrible names, assaulted field workers, and even molested young peasant girls. One time they tortured their housemaid by locking her in a wooden shed with a nest of bumblebees. Tejan found their behavior amusing and dismissed the victims by offering money to cover up his sons' mistakes.

Belan, who started off with thirty-five acres of good, fertile land, now owned over eighty acres, some of which he leased and some on which he grew wheat, barley, maize, sugar cane, and cotton in alternate seasons. He had bought another farm with a grand house on it from a wealthy family who had emigrated to Canada. Belan didn't want to miss on the opportunity. The house was situated on five acres of farmland, with a paved driveway joining the main road. The main house was bordered by tall eucalyptus trees and had two front and back entrances. Wrought-iron gates, which were always kept shut, provided the security for the family.

Belan and Shanti traveled to the state of Rajasthan in northwest India, hundreds of miles away, to attend a relative's daughter's wedding. From there, they bought fine furniture and rugs. Belan had a very good taste in home furnishing. He appreciated good rugs, dhurries, and other handwoven tapestries. Their home was one of the finest in the fifty villages around them. They had dozens of servants and regular workers who helped in the fields. There was an entire block of rooms just for the housemaids and their families. The house, which grew to three times its original size, constantly demanded upkeep, paint jobs, and small repairs. It had several rooms, including a Bedak (Formal drawing room), where male guests or out-of-town people visited for business deals, such as buying or selling cattle or other farming equipment. Most people conducted their business outside the family home. It was rare for people to announce their arrival at the gate, and when guests arrived unannounced, they were greeted with respect.

Belan and Shanti were a very well-respected couple— the only couple who could read and write in the area. Landlords and ladies from the neighboring villages came to the house in their carriages when they needed a letter sent to their relatives or daughters. They trusted Shanti to help them over the village teacher or postman. There was a constant flow of families seeking financial help. Belan tried to help them as much as he could. Many traded services with him, as they could not pay him back in money.

When an expert village roofer needed money for his daughter's wedding, Belan got him to build the cow sheds on his farm. Never did he take advantage of a poor soul. His wife also helped the villagers in time of need. She often helped them out with food, clothes, and necessary bedding if they needed, but she much preferred to teach them how to manage their households. She taught women how to sew and reuse their old worn-out clothes for their children; she taught them how to do chores more efficiently. Belan ran his farm like a sergeant's drill—he gave his workers good tools to work, good food to eat, and enough rest, but he did not tolerate laziness or people who whined too much. The family did not allow any kind of malicious talk among their workers. It was a happy home.

Tejan visited his mother occasionally, begging for forgiveness and cursing and blaming his wife for his misfortunes, but he was not genuine. It was just an excuse; the real reason was to spy on his brother. His brother's success had made him very suspicious and insecure. His efforts to extract information from his mother left him exhausted. Jealousy and deceit were written all over his face. His mother's advice to take a wife went from one ear to the other.

It also was an elegant home, with modern furniture, a large fireplace, and a large portrait on the wall of Belan's father wearing a turban and holding a rifle. In the dining area there was a large carved wooden table with a dozen chairs, placed under a wrought-iron chandelier with a dozen candles. There were also two large end tables for serving food. Each room had at least four windows with wooden slats and wrought-iron bars through them. Nothing except air could pass through them. All windows opened on both sides of the room, facing the veranda and the inner courtyard. There were twenty-four pillars around the inner and outer verandas. Right in the middle of the courtyard was a water well, surrounded by a paved floor. All around the well was a carefully manicured lawn, bordered by flowerbeds. It was such a pretty sound to hear the water tumbling when the housemaids drew water from the well. There was also an open trench from which the water flowed into a large concrete tub. Water flowed in two different directions—toward the back of the kitchen for cleaning and washing, and toward the sleeping quarters of the family. Open bathhouses had tightly knotted bamboo sticks around them for privacy.

Shanti had an indoor and outdoor kitchen, which she used all year-round. The outdoor kitchen had an earthen tandoor (an oven), as well as an open-fire stove with a chimney. The indoor kitchen had plenty of light with plenty of workspace. A big storage room attached to the indoor kitchen accommodated all nonperishable items like wheat, rice, lentils, beans, oils, pickles, salt, and honey. Everything was kept in tightly sealed metal canisters. Dairy products, such as milk, butter, and cheese, were kept in an open-air pantry in a shady dark place. Plenty of fresh vegetables and fruit were picked daily. On the east side of the house were vines of cucumbers, zucchini, pumpkins, and tomatoes. There was a big banyan tree in the backyard where kids played during the day. Fruit trees, like mangoes, papayas, and lychees, along the house wall were loaded with fruit. Another well-kept vegetable garden was near the outdoor kitchen, along with a water station with hand pump that Shanti had cleverly designed. It didn't just come in handy while cooking and cleaning the dishes; it also was very practical for the vegetable garden. The outdoor kitchen extended further than the veranda. Outside the parameters of the main house was an outer house that consisted of barracks for the servants and bath houses for them. Beyond that, was where all the animals were kept in a partly covered yard. Several milking cows, goats, and hens filled the barn.

The entire house was so practically designed that it was easy to manage. Everything had its place and its need. A little mud fence that surrounded the outdoor kitchen kept the house pets away. A mango tree in the inner courtyard gave plenty of shade at noon for kids to play and eat. Shanti looked after the home and took care of her mother-in-law until the day she died.

Mean-spirited Tejan, who could not stomach his brother's success, openly expressed his dislike for his brother. He often shared his grievances with villagers, accusing his brother of embarrassing his family. Belan worked hard in his fields, and that troubled his brother. He felt that Belan was deliberately trying to shame and dishonor him and his ancestral family by slaving away with servants in the fields. According to him, respectable landlords were supposed to live a good lifestyle, and field work was supposed to be left for the lower caste. Tejan using profane language when addressing others, and that was proof enough for villagers to judge who was a better person. His lack of compassion and respect for others was not new, but his jealousy and animosity for his brother shocked the whole community. He was an embarrassment—a shady characterless man.

There was no dialogue between the brothers. Tejan's animosity grew so strong that he hired armed men to attack his brother. The attack took place when four men hid in his sugar cane field. They came from behind and covered his face with a burlap sack. They tried to strangle him and kicked his stomach until he fell on the ground. Then other two jumped on top of him, twisting the sack around his neck. Belan, however, was an ex-military man and had been well trained in combat, and he still was as strong as a bull. He could easily tackle six to eight men at once. It took him few seconds to register and react, but when he responded with fists, all four offenders fell away from him. He removed the sack from his face and pounded them with his fists and kicks until they cried in pain, begging for his forgiveness.

Totally puzzled by this bizarre attack, Belan questioned the men by grabbing their necks and demanding an explanation. He grabbed a rope from the sugar cane bundle nearby and tied up their bodies. He was planning to hand them over to the constable when all four men cried to save their skin and admitted that it was Tejan who had sent them and paid them to attack Belan. Hearing this, Belan's heart sank with sadness. He could not have imagined his brother stooping so low. When he dragged all four men over to his brother's house and demanded the explanation, Tejan and his sons were in a state of shock. Tejan put his arm around his brother and pretended as if he was totally oblivious to what was going on. When Belan reported that the men had confessed, Tejan went ballistic. He approached the men and started whipping them with his leather leash. Then he begged Belan not to believe them. He kept beating them until they changed their story. One of them invented a story, and others went along with him. Their fabricated story was that they were just passing by the sugar cane field when they decided to take a break. Belan just came from nowhere and started whipping them. The same man went on to say that Belan misunderstood that they had mentioned his brother's name.

At that point, Belan was ready to take the leash in his own hands so he could teach them a lesson. Tejan promised to take care of the goons and tried to convince Belan that he was a victim of a conspiracy, and some of his enemies were taking advantage of the situation. He continued to beg Belan to believe him, but Belan knew the truth.

Belan was saddened that his brother wanted to harm him. Stories of his brother's using forceful ways to gain from others were known to all, but seeing him beat up his own men with a leash was proof of his evilness. He didn't want to share the incident with his mother. He could not, however, keep his torn clothes and bleeding nose a secret from his wife. Shanti was terrified to learn that her family's life was in danger again. She trusted that her husband could take care of himself, but she became paranoid about Puran. She couldn't remain silent about it and shared her fears with her mother-in-law. Belan's mother was furious and wanted to confront Tejan. Still in a state of shock, Belan hadn't realized that he was hurt on his forehead and that his forearms were covered with bruises and scratches. He kept his mother from going to Tejan's house, but he respected her sentiments. He had seen his brother and his sons lie through their teeth, and there was nothing his mother could do to shame him.

Belan called a family meeting, and all servants were asked to be careful about the safety and security of Puran. Belan didn't say anything about his attack or name his brother, but the servants had already guessed it. Belan's mother sympathized with her daughter-in-law and advised her to be more vigilant about Puran.

Puran's safety became family's priority again. The attackers had confirmed that Tejan and his sons had their eyes on his wealth. Daughters were not considered a threat, since girls didn't inherit the land. Laws were not in favor of women's rights, especially property laws, which were ridiculously unfair. According to the law, if the family didn't have a son, the land automatically went to the nearest uncle and his sons. Powerful and greedy landlords tried to abduct or kill anyone who came in the way of benefitting the land. It wasn't until much later that the Hindu Women's Right to Property Act was put in place, along with other legal reforms.

Belan's suspicions became real when he found out that his greedy and lazy brother had lost half of his land, some due to mismanagement and some due to a foolish decision to lease his land to some crooks from other villages. He sold one-third of his land to renovate and modernize the family house, just to keep up with his brother. His flamboyant lifestyle, his enjoyment of foreign whiskeys, and his entertaining crooks soon landed him in debt. The sons followed suit and soon ran out of money. The family needed more and more cash, and Tejan ended up selling his assets, such as family heirlooms and horses and cattle.

The farmers who were leasing the land from him were flourishing. They were hardworking people who knew the value of a fertile land, and they made huge profits from their crops. Belan, being a farmer, was familiar with the profit margin. He admired the farmers who leased his brother's land for their attempts to get rich, but the farmers avoided Belan out of guilt.

Belan didn't trust anyone around his family except his loyal servants. Any stranger lurking around was brought in front of him, questioned, and punished if needed. Trained guard dogs were sent for their protection. An ex-military man was hired as Puran's bodyguard after another terrible incident—snakes were let loose in Puran's closet.

Shanti didn't normally allow strangers or vendors inside the house, but it had been raining, and the poor vendor who came to the door was drenched. Shanti kindly gave the old woman dry clothes and allowed her into her home to change. She had no clue of any danger from her, but later that day, when snakes were found in

Puran's closet, it was clear the old vendor had carried them in her basket. Belan sent his men in search of the woman but to no avail.

A few months later, there was another incident when a newly hired male servant from Tejan's household disguised himself as a hakim—a medicine man—and came to the house in an attempt to poison Puran. One of the housemaids recognized him and suspected him of foul play. She informed Shanti immediately, who had him caught and tied up for interrogation later. Belan rushed home as soon as he heard about another senseless act of vengeance against his son. Belan took his pistol and threatened to shoot the man on the spot if he didn't tell him what he was doing there. The hakim admitted that Tejan had sent him to poison Puran. Belan felt as if he had been stabbed in his chest.

After much debate and deliberation with the family and other members of the community, Belan dragged his brother to the Panchayat, the group of chosen respected member of community who acted as judges who made decisions and resolved disputes, so the members could rectify the situation with his brother. Belan was a peace-loving man, but Tejan had crossed all boundaries. He had to be punished for his heinous crimes. Belan didn't usually lose his temper but at that moment, nothing would have felt better than slitting his brother's throat.

The Panchayat sat on the designated date, and the entire village was present. The brothers sat across from one another. It wasn't a common practice for families to go to court for such disputes. In most villages, the Panchayat made decisions, and those decisions were honored. It was true that the Panchayat was formed by members who were highly respected and honorable because of their fair and honest opinions. They were chosen for their honorable traits, such as discernment and integrity. But the post-war economy of the nation had changed the definition of moral values. It was a matter of surviving the hunger. The Panchayat members in Belan's village were old men who were either hard of hearing or dictated to by others.

Belan described the incidents and accused his brother of acts of cruelty. Tejan, in response to his brother's accusations, asked if he had any proof. None of the perpetrators Tejan had hired would admit to any wrongdoing—they all feared Tejan's wrath. Tejan himself denied every accusation against him in the presence of Panchayat. Nothing conclusive came out of the meeting. Disappointed and crushed, Belan lost his faith in the system. He looked in the eyes of same men who had admitted their guilt to him. He knew they were being manipulated and controlled by his cunning brother. He felt helpless and defeated. Ironically, he was in better control of the situation in the war with enemies than at home. The meaning of honor, discipline, respect, integrity, and humility was unknown to these lowly men.

Belan realized that his own brother, Tejan, was his worst enemy, and he didn't know how to fight him. Cruelty toward a harmless child was beyond Belan's comprehension. The sarcastic smile on Tejan's face was proof enough that he was guilty.

1925—India

PURAN'S TROUBLES

Puran had a mosquito bite on his leg that turned into an abscess, and eventually the infection got into the shinbone. Constant pain in his leg made Puran limp as he walked, especially in winter. None of the home remedies that were tried had any effect on it. Puran's abscess had become incurable. Hakims and village doctors had tried various turmeric poultices and rare tree-root powders. One hakim even tried cat's claw, as it enhanced the immune response and possessed antibacterial properties. People in the villages believed a person got sick because he offended a spirit or divinity with his actions, but even Shanti's prayers and fasts didn't help Puran either.

Belan had to seek proper medical treatment for his son's incurable abscess. His mother would help him wrap his leg in bandages to protect it from dirty rainwater. It was getting to the point where the abscess was constantly bleeding or full of puss. Some ignorant people in the village stayed away from Puran out of fear of contracting a contagious disease.

Belan was very concerned about his son's leg; he wanted Puran to see a city doctor. Suraj had also pleaded with Puran in letters to seek proper treatment. After several nonresponsive home treatments, Belan asked his son Suraj to locate a good doctor in the city. Suraj made all arrangements with the help of his senior officers. The army doctors looked at his brother's leg and immediately admitted Puran to the proper facility under the care of the British surgeon general. Doctors had diagnosed gangrene; the only treatment was amputation of his right leg below the knee. The situation was very grave; there was no time to think, as the decision had to be made quickly.

There was no question that it was more important to save Puran's life than his leg. Obviously, it was shocking, and Belan cried on his younger son's shoulder, but he remained calm and strong for Puran. It took the doctors and nurses many hours to convince Puran that it was the only thing that could be done. Puran didn't understand the seriousness of gangrene or why it could not be cured. The doctors had to assure him that he could have a full normal life after amputation, but without it, he would surely die. Finally, Puran agreed to the operation.

The day of their return home from the city was a sad day. Belan visualized the scene at home, as he knew this was going to shock Shanti, who didn't know yet what had happened. When they arrived at home, Belan jumped off the horse cart and rushed to the house, leaving Puran sitting on the cart bench with the blanket over his lap. Belan called for his wife and explained the situation. After a few minutes, he helped Puran out of the cart, with the help of servants, and took him straight to his room. Shanti burst into tears as she hugged Puran. There were waterworks and hugs from his grandmother too.

The next morning, the servants were advised of the special attention needed for Puran's care. Certain servants were assigned for certain tasks in an effort to make Puran comfortable. Both parents tried to be very positive, and they encouraged their son to look at the bright side. They reminded him that it was a blessing that he was alive and well, but Puran didn't think his life was worth living. Every day, he woke up with intense bitterness and depression.

Watching him try to balance himself on his crutches pained his parents. They loved their son and had great plans for his marriage to one of their neighboring landlord's daughter. They could not hide their disappointment when the message came through from the girl's family, breaking the alliance. They understood the situation and tried not to take it personally. Any parent with plenty of wealth and a beautiful daughter would want the best man for their daughter. Apparently, Puran wasn't the best for their daughter anymore.

Word of the broken alliance reached Puran's ears, but Belan and Shanti told Puran to disregard the information; they wanted to buy time in which to find a better match for him. Time went by, but no match came forward for him. Puran sensed the tension and spent more and more time with men around the village, just to hide his disappointment. His parents could not think of anything to do for his anxiety and depression. His mean uncle and his cousins spotted him drinking with the servants on a couple of occasions. They took the opportunity to execute their conniving scheme of pretending to take him under their wing. Later, Puran's misjudgment and misunderstanding of the matter cost him his life.

Puran had relentlessly blamed his father and brother for losing his leg. His uncle and his cousins somehow had manipulated him into believing that his parents did not want him to get married. Tejan knew what he had to do to win Puran's confidence. Once Tejan established that, Puran trusted him fully and kept the relationship a secret from his father. Tejan made his move; he became overly loving toward his nephew—it was love that Puran felt his own father deprived him of. Puran had no clue about the scheme his uncle and his cousins were planning. They discreetly introduced him to opium in the form of medicine administered by their hakim, to help Puran with his leg pain. They also promised to find a suitable match for him, since the cousins were experts on such matters.

Puran also believed that his parents cared about his brother, Suraj, more than they cared about him, as they constantly worried about Suraj while he was away from home. Puran become more and more aloof with his parents. He kept to himself at home or stayed away from home in the company of his cousins, Mangal and Shankar. Belan was very worried but was helpless; his son had shut him out. Tejan had won; he had his nephew under his influence and was abusing him without his knowledge.

Tejan's various strategies to win over his nephew had driven a wedge between Puran and his father. First, Tejan begged his brother for forgiveness and asked his mother to come live at his house—it had been years since he had spoken to his mother. He even beat up his sons in front of Belan's entire family, blaming his misfortune on his stupid wife, who had left them. He was overly dramatic and grabbed a machete lying nearby in a basket full of fresh-cut hay. He started swinging the machete violently about his sons, while cursing and threatening to chop off their hands for harming his nephew Puran. Belan stopped him from swinging the machete. For a moment, he truly believed Tejan was remorseful, but that moment didn't last long. His mother was doubtful too and refused to go to Tejan's house. She strongly advised Belan to be careful about his brother, for she knew her son well.

Puran, however, was totally taken in by his uncle's overly dramatized plea for forgiveness. He felt embarrassed by his father's attitude of mistrust toward his older brother, embarrassed that his father would not accept his uncle's apology. Puran tried to compensate for his father by being extra friendly and trusting. He no longer felt threatened by his uncle or his cousins; in fact, the cousins were being very kind and protective toward him. Belan warned his son against the dangerous situation he was putting himself under by trusting them, for he was suspicious of their sick minds. Tejan and his sons knew they were being watched and that one little accident that harmed Puran would be a serious mistake. Eventually, things were calm; the family needed the time to restore the trust.

Mangal had introduced Puran to the town whores, and Shankar gave him a taste of opium. Both opium and women took care of him for a short while, but Puran's conscience nagged at him in his sleep. It pierced his heart when his mother turned her face away from him in disgust. Her love and respect was replaced by mistrust and indignation. Puran had not forgotten how his mother had nursed him to health from childhood fevers, how she had waited by the gate on his return from school, how she had sung nursery rhymes to soothe him to sleep, and how she had taught him chess and let him win. All those images of his mother in his mind wounded him. Shanti adored and missed her son who was so attached to her. Puran had been her shield in her husband's absence. She was disappointed in his choice of lifestyle, but she felt sorry for him and understood his pain.

Even though both parents pretended they didn't care about the rumors they'd heard about Puran, they knew the rumors were true. There was enough evidence in their son's behavior to prove he was under the influence of opium, and the snickering going on behind their backs confirmed that their son was up to no good. Puran's aggressive nature was very new to his parents. The way Puran demanded money shocked Belan, who became very fearful that Tejan would soon convince Puran to split the land, just like he did some years ago.

Belan started to have nightmares. He had built an empire but was losing his son. It seemed history was going to repeat itself. To keep Puran calm, Belan kept giving money to his son without any question, even though he knew it was paying for Puran's bad habits. Village people were sympathetic toward the family and guessed the real culprit behind the change in Puran's behavior. Belan and his wife never accused or confronted the other family. They tried to put sense in their own son, but he refused to listen to them.

Puran would not admit it to his parents, but he used opium not just for the pain in his leg but for the pain in his heart as well. Puran wanted a wife and a family of his own, but his cousins reminded him daily that his chances of getting married and having a family were slim. Puran realized that under different circumstances, he could have been good at farming and a great help to his father as a landlord. Deep down, Puran did look up to his parents. As a kid, he often wished for a wife like his mother, a well-respected, beautiful girl with whom he could share a life. He was aware of the shame he had brought upon family, but it was impossible to undo the damage. To let his family down was the worst feeling he could have had.

Both of his younger sisters came to visit him after his leg amputation. They supported him and cried with him, but when they heard about his new lifestyle, they were disgusted. Later, both sent messages saying that they never wanted to see him again, for he had caused great grief to their parents.

Puran cried alone at nights; he refused to be with the women his cousins brought him. During the day, he spent his time in his fields, roaming around, giving orders, checking on servants, and avoiding his father at all times. In the evening, he asked for his meals in his room. For some reason, he had started suspecting that his cousins really did not want him to settle down. He knew Mangal was married but still fooled around with whores and undesirable characters. Puran also wondered how his uncle and cousins would benefit from his downfall. Did they really expect that his brother, Suraj, would not return home? Their conspiracy was too complex for his simple mind.

This particular incident happened when his mean cousins played a cruel prank on him. They had manipulated their village matchmaker to suggest a good match for Puran and, if successful, promised him a hefty reward. The greedy matchmaker considered Puran's position and went hunting for a bride. Puran was very hopeful and excited. A month later, he received a message to meet up with the matchmaker at the train station. He was clearly excited to see his future bride, who was accompanying the matchmaker. He thought of asking his mother to come along so she could bless their union, but he feared that his mother might not agree with the methods he had used, so he kept it a secret.

When he arrived at the train station, he saw a plain-looking girl sitting on the bench with the matchmaker. As he walked toward her, he sensed that the girl was looking straight ahead at nothing in particular. She neither flinched nor showed any sign that she saw him approach, and she didn't respond when he said hello. Puran signaled the matchmaker to speak to him in private. He pulled him aside and whispered harshly, "What is wrong with that girl? Why is she here if she won't acknowledge me?"

The matchmaker was stunned. "Surely you knew … did your cousins not tell you?" He lowered his voice and spoke in a rush. "They asked me to find someone suitable. They spoke to the girl's family prior to this arrangement and promised that you would marry their daughter. The girl's parents have already sent the dowry to your cousins. She is here to marry you."

There was no going back; the girl was literally married to Puran, and her parents would not accept her back. Puran felt ridiculed and cheated. If he had been physically able to fight, he would have torn into his cousins. But now, there was nothing he could do. He felt sick as he imagined the entire village laughing at the newly married couple. He could not accept that. His life was getting more and more complicated. He turned and walked away from the station, with the matchmaker calling after him. The girl, of course, was unaware of the scene that had taken place, and Puran was glad of that.

His cousins' mocking faces floated through his mind. He couldn't believe they had been so devious. He kept walking along the train track, even as he heard the noise of a train approaching from farther down the track. The sound became deafening as the train was almost upon him, and suddenly, Puran jumped in front of the oncoming train. His body was dragged down the track under the carriage. It was unrecognizable.

It had been three years since Suraj last had seen his father and brother. After the surgery, he had dropped them off at the train station, where Puran sat in the wheelchair, waiting for a porter to assist him onto the train. In September 1925, Suraj received a telegram, informing him that his older brother, Puran, had been in a terrible accident and had passed away. Puran was a year older than Suraj, but at the age of twenty-five, Puran was dead. Suraj knew the responsibilities lay with him concerning the funeral and other important tasks. Knowing the situation of his parents—that they relied on him for support—he decided to go home. His senior officers were very sympathetic and permitted him to go home for few weeks.

The situation at home was worse than Suraj had imagined. Even though his father had been writing to him on regular basis, informing him of the news at home and in the village, Suraj had no clue of the extent of his uncle's cruel tactics. His parents, whom he hadn't seen in three years, had gotten so old in that time; he couldn't believe his eyes. His brother had been the victim of a cruel joke played by his uncle and cousins. Funeral arrangements were made, and both of his sisters came back to lend their support. No matter how much everybody cried, however, nothing seemed to lessen the pain in their hearts.

Belan was haunted by images of his son's lifeless body sprawled across the platform. His son had died in vain, without warning, and without a chance to say good-bye. Belan's grief was unbearable. The entire village was seething with hate and anger toward Tejan and his sons. Villagers demanded justice, but Belan and Shanti couldn't muster the strength to deal with such issues. Their aspirations and dreams for their son's success and happiness were distorted and unmet by the cruel reality of life. Belan wished he could hold his son in his embrace and tell him that he understood his pain, that he loved him very much, that he was sorry for being disappointed in him, and that if he could turn the clock back, he would accept his son with all his faults. Unspeakable pain, helplessness, frustration, and sadness were visible on Belan's and Shanti's faces, but although they divulged their anger and disappointment to God, they refused to discuss their pain with each other. Sudden grief attacks that continued to sneak up and surprise them equally from time to time made Belan questioned himself, wondering if he was a good father. One son had been sent away to the army, and the other had ended his own life.

It had been six weeks since Suraj had arrived home in an attempt to make it better for his family while he was dealing with his own grief. Deeply inflicted wounds weren't going to get healed as easily. He didn't like to mope around the place. His emotional outbursts were not known to anyone, as he hid them well. Being of a practical nature, he continued to work in the fields along with the workers, and he rode his horse to the far end of the land to see that the crops were watered properly, making sure the workers were not sneaking off early or being lazy. One evening as he sat with his mother, having a heart-to-heart conversation, she said very softly, "Please come home, Suraj. Come home and settle down with a wife." He could do nothing else but pity his mother. It was a subtle hint that she was very lonely.

1927—India

A Marriage Proposal

The prospect of a bride for her son gave Shanti a little hope in life. She knew it was not the right time, but she had to ask Suraj to consider it. Perhaps on his next visit, he could get engaged. She had someone in mind for him, a daughter of a landlord in the neighboring village, but the girl's family needed to know if the alliance was acceptable to Suraj, as other respectable families were interested in her. The girl in question, Maya, was not only pretty but smart too. She was the youngest and the only daughter. Her four brothers and their wives adored her. Her mother was a fine lady who instilled good morals and taught her daughter to be ladylike.

As a young girl, Maya played with her brothers and grew up playing sports. Unaware of her beauty and attractiveness, she behaved more like a tomboy who never looked in the mirror. Her brothers and other boys never thought of Maya as pretty, because she was very competitive and beat the boys in their own games—they hated to lose. While other girls her age learned embroidery, cooking, and household chores, Maya climbed trees and rode bicycles. Her mother became very concerned of her boyish flair and wanted her husband's help to tame the girl. Her father didn't mind his young daughter's scraped knees and elbows, since she was not marriageable age.

Maya's sense of humor and bluntness didn't amuse older women, as she would imitate their whining and complaining about life. Her knack of telling long tales and keeping her listeners interested was terrific. Some women didn't like their daughters to be influenced by her but overall, Maya was loved by all. She was witty and kind at heart, as well as respectful, but not afraid to speak her mind. As Maya grew up, she became a beautiful young lady who was physically attractive and emotionally thoughtful. She was mature, sensible, and very capable, and her parents decided that Maya was ready for marriage. Her parents were very proud and humbled by the fact that there were lots of choices for good husbands out there. It was when Maya's family attended a relative's wedding in Suraj's village that Shanti first saw Maya. Shanti was certain that if Suraj could see Maya, he would fall in love with her.

Their neighboring landlord's daughter's wedding— the wedding that Maya and her family were attending— followed the old traditions, and so gifts of food, clothing, and bedding were sent to the family by relatives and neighbors. Milk, cheese, butter, raw sugar, oil for frying, and sacks of onions and potatoes started arriving at the family home. Basic ingredients were needed for making traditional snacks and sweets for the guests who were arriving for the wedding ahead of time. Borrowing large pots and pans to cook and even borrowing bed cots from neighbors was common practice, as all families joined in the celebration. Women eagerly awaited the wedding celebrations—it was a lot of work, but it was fun. Shanti also presented herself at the family's home with generous gifts. She had half a dozen servants carrying sacks full of ingredients.

The wedding house was full of guests, with older women getting ready for the traditional rituals and young girls getting dressed in beautiful outfits, fixing each other's hair and jewelry, and giggling nonstop in anticipation of the henna ceremony. In the hustle and bustle of it all, Maya didn't know which way to go first. It was her cousin who was getting married, and she needed Maya by her side, but Maya's grandmother needed Maya to fetch her cane, and someone else wanted something else from her. An elderly lady of the house sent Maya with refreshments to the room full of guests—including Shanti—who had arrived for the wedding. Shanti watched Maya handle the guests with courtesy and competence. The girl's charismatic personality, her mannerisms, and her confident look totally matched her exterior beauty. Her poised figure, her skin complexion, her eyes, and her long braided hair—every bit of Maya was lovely. Shanti was amused by Maya's full-hearted laughter and her candor. She was drawn to Maya like a magnet. Shanti secretly prayed that her son would agree to this alliance, knowing that Suraj, who had a taste of city life, might not settle for a girl from the village.

The next evening, without hesitation, Shanti asked Suraj to accompany her to the pre-wedding ceremonies. Reluctantly, Suraj agreed to escort his mother. The bride's brothers knew Suraj well and made him feel welcome, but poor Suraj got tricked into helping the family with chores. He avoided entering a courtyard full of females; he was petrified. He wasn't shy or introverted, but being face-to-face with so many giddy girls at once could make any man nervous. It was later when Suraj was delivering sheets and pillows in the dark storeroom that he knocked someone off the ladder. That someone was Maya, who was up on the ladder, placing baskets of sweets on a higher shelf. She landed right in Suraj's arms but dropped the entire contents of the basket on the floor. Both collided on the floor, with Maya on top of Suraj. Infuriated and irritated, Maya cursed under her breath and quickly removed herself from top of him. She grabbed her veil, straightened herself out, collected the damaged sweets in her basket, and ran out of the storeroom before anyone could see her.

Suraj stayed on the floor and was totally baffled, half intoxicated, and a little excited. He felt as if an electric current had passed through his body, and he found himself smiling. Maya's face in his eyes, her body in his arms, and one of her gold hoop earrings in his hand had hypnotized him. He heard someone call his name. He fixed himself up and left the storeroom. There was a lot of clatter coming from the women in the inner courtyard—clapping and singing, followed by thunderous noise of laughter. Suraj wondered if the girl had told them everything. He had never been to an event like this before. Men in outer courtyard were roasting chickens in the tandoors while drinking rum. Some young boys were trying to climb the wall, which separated the two courtyards, just to take a sneak peak at the girls dancing. Men weren't allowed in the inner courtyard.

One young boy asked Suraj, "Could I climb on your shoulders to see the girls?"

"Very well," Suraj agreed, "on one condition—you must try to spot a girl with one earring."

The young boy laughed. "I will try." He climbed on Suraj's shoulders and scanned the group of girls. "They all have both earrings or none," he announced. "Wait … except one."

Suraj held his breath and asked the boy what she was wearing. It was dark in the storeroom, and he had not paid any attention to her clothes. He knew he would recognize her immediately if he came face-to-face with her. Suraj instructed the boy, "Try to get the girl's attention and ask her to come to the wall." The sweet and harmless kid whistled to Maya to get her attention. She immediately approached the wall, and as she looked up at the young boy, she heard Suraj speak from behind the wall. "What is your name?" he asked.

"Who are you?" she demanded.

Suraj gently put the boy on the ground and shooed him off. He spoke to Maya in a hushed voice. "I have your gold hoop."

Maya touched her both ears and found one of the hoops missing. She gasped and said, "Throw it over the wall,"

"No, meet me behind the storeroom," he said.

Maya was amused by his trick, but she agreed to see him. She was quick to find out from her cousin who had been in the storeroom earlier with sheets and pillows. Her cousin laughed and said, "That was Suraj. You remember Shanti, the lady who was interested in you for her son? Suraj is her son."

Maya remembered Shanti from the previous evening. She had liked her a lot. After collecting all the information about Suraj and his family, Maya and her cousin both headed toward the storeroom to meet with Suraj, Maya being very thankful for the girlhood pact. Girls confided in each other more easily than boys did.

Few minutes later when Maya found an opportunity to get away from singing and dancing, she dragged her cousin sister with her and slipped away, making a bathroom excuse. Suraj was already waiting there for her. He was alone. There was a gorgeous sunset across the green fields and a light breeze. There was something about the darkest stage of twilight in the evening, with enough light in the sky, that made the universe so romantic. Suraj saw her coming toward him in the company of another girl, which he wasn't pleased about, but then, he had not asked her to come alone; he couldn't blame her. Maya looked even more beautiful in that evening sun, with rosy cheeks from heat or exhaustion. Suraj greeted both girls and then politely asked the cousin, "Could I have a private word with your friend?"

The girl nodded with a smile and walked away, leaving them alone. Maya called after her cousin, but Suraj was quick to allay her fears of being alone with him. "Look," he said, showing her the gold hoop in his hand.

Maya didn't expect him to outsmart her so easily by getting rid of her cousin. "Smart move," she told him.

"Smart girl," Suraj responded, pointing to her cousin, indicating that she was smart to leave them. Suraj couldn't take his eyes off Maya. He wanted to talk to her and to get to know her. "What's your name?" he asked, ending the awkward silence.

"I'll tell you my name when you give me my hoop."

Suraj looked at the gold hoop for few seconds, reviewing his situation. When would he have another chance to be in possession of something that belonged to the girl he was falling for so fast? He handed the hoop to her.

Maya smiled and said, "My name is Maya."

Suraj nodded; he liked the name Maya. As Maya turned to go, Suraj extended his arm against the wall, stopping her from leaving. "Don't you want to know my name?" he asked.

Maya crossed her arms across her chest and examined him thoroughly. There was a gleam in her eyes and bright smile on her lips as she informed him, "I know your name, your age, what you do for a living, and where you live. I've also met your mother."

Suraj's jaw hit the floor after hearing this. *This girl has done her homework*, he thought. *She is smarter and way ahead of me.* "How long will you be visiting the village? Can I see you again?"

Maya was blushing; no one had ever asked that of her before. Village boys would never dare to seek a girl in this fashion. "You'll see me at the wedding tomorrow ... if you're going to be there."

"I wasn't planning on attending," he admitted, "but now I would like to, if I can find something decent to wear." He had not brought any of the traditional outfits worn by men for the wedding. He generally wore pants and shirts.

Maya's eyes twinkled as she said, "You better hurry along." And she left in a flurry.

Belan was home alone in the courtyard, listening to the radio, when Suraj returned and pulled up a chair next to his father. "May I speak with you?" he asked. He always looked up to his father for his opinions and suggestions. Now, he needed to discuss some serious issues like his career, his marriage, and his new responsibilities and expectations at home, now that his brother was gone. Suraj also was very concerned about his father's health and wanted to address that.

They sat there for hours—finding solutions, choosing different options, and finally coming to the conclusion that it was best for Suraj to stay in the army, for he had a very bright future. Suraj had come too far in his career to quit now. At a captain's rank in the Indian army, he was fully committed to his country and to his unit. The army offered a lot of benefits and huge pensions, and the army made it easy for officers to keep their families with them. Suraj didn't like the idea of his parents living by themselves now that they were getting old. His grandmother's health had deteriorated so much in the last few months that she needed full-time care. They discussed the option of leasing the land to some young farmers to lessen the burden for Belan as well as getting a regular income from their land. Suraj had suggested setting up a home in the city, where all facilities were readily available for elderly parents, but Belan quickly dismissed that option.

"Life in city is too hectic for your mother and me—and your grandmother, too. Besides, it would not be dignified for the family to rent a place to live." He shook his head vehemently, "No, I could not get used to the city life at my age. I love being on the farm, where I can breathe fresh air and where I know my people." He did agree, however, that he and Shanti would visit the doctors in city once a year for regular checkups and to receive proper medicine. Belan then said to his son, "As for you, get married, and take your wife along with you. I'm not afraid of my brother anymore. God has already punished him for his crimes." Tejan too had lost his younger son, Shankar, to an overdose of opium in the month after Puran's death. Belan knew that Tejan was easing his grief with drinking, to the point that he appeared drunk all the time. The villainous duo got a taste of their own medicine; they too felt the pain and hurt of losing their loved one. Their friends disappeared as fast as their money, leaving them distraught and desolate. Shanti continued to send food and presents for the children on special occasions.

"Would you speak to Maya's father about her hand in marriage?" Suraj asked his father.

"I will do that," Belan agreed, "if you promise to visit home more regularly."

On the morning of the neighbor's wedding, Suraj got up early to keep his father company on the rounds to his fields. They rode their horses to check on the progress of the harvesting, and they met up with group of men and women picking cotton. Belan got off his horse and tied him up in the shade of a tree. Suraj followed his father and listened to the instructions he was giving to the foreman. Suraj was astonished at the knowledge his father had about crops, soil fertilizers, tractors, and other essential tools needed for modern agricultural methods. He was proud that his father was a leader to the other farmers in their area. Until this moment, Suraj had not appreciated the resources his father had. Now, he humbly appreciated the value of his inheritance.

Belan was trying to show his son the ropes of being a landlord, and Suraj was giving his father his undivided attention. Belan was pleased when his son had agreed to settle down. He had shared this exciting news with Shanti, who was thrilled and couldn't wait to make arrangements with Maya's family. Delighted by the thought of a new bride, new life, and new hope, Shanti and Belan saw the light at the end of the tunnel. Now, both father and son headed home for breakfast with new optimism in their hearts and smiles on their faces.

Shanti had her men's clothes neatly laid out in their rooms. They got dressed and then all left for the wedding ceremony in their horse cart. The wedding mandap—a porch-like structure with an ornate gateway—was beautifully decorated for the baraat, the procession led by groom on a horseback. The baraat had not arrived, but the bride's family was waiting at the gate to receive guests with flower garlands.

Suraj looked handsome in his princely outfit. His eyes searched for Maya; he expected her to be with the bride. He realized that he didn't recognize many people; he felt like a stranger in his own village. He offered to help out with the arrangements for the wedding ceremony. The bride's brothers were busy with setting up the food tables. Some men were busy setting up the marquee and floor coverings. The baraat was supposed to have refreshments in the pergola before the ceremony started.

Belan called to Suraj, telling him to come and meet one of his acquaintances from the neighboring village. Suraj wished the older man a good day, and Belan whispered to his son, informing him that the man he had just met was Maya's father. Suraj hoped he had made a good impression on him. Suraj was unaware of secret signals between Maya's family and his own parents. His innocence about the whole matchmaking scheme made him look even more striking to Maya.

In the city, he had been to a friend's wedding, and the couple had walked around the fire a few times and exchanged garlands. There were hardly a dozen guests in the hotel where the ceremony took place. There was no singing, no drums, no baraat, no ongoing laughter and ceremonies for days before. Suraj definitely liked the village wedding far better than the city wedding. It was much more fun—or was it fun because Maya was there?

The night before, Maya's cousin had told Maya about Suraj's older brother and how their cousins' wicked plan had caused Puran to take his own life. Maya also learned that Suraj's mother had handled the entire household in her husband's absence and the painful separation from her sons. Maya commended her for the way she coped with her grief after losing her son and how she looked after her ailing mother-in-law. She knew Suraj had couple of sisters who were happily married with families of their own. They too lived at home with their in-laws while their husbands were away on duty.

After the ceremony, Maya spotted Suraj in the marquee, having lunch with a group of men. Maya was part of the group of girls who had hidden the groom's shoes—she loved this traditional wedding game played by the bridesmaids. Now it was bridesmaids versus groomsmen, as both parties tried to negotiate a price for the return of the groom's shoes. The girls wanted one hundred rupees, but the groomsmen were only willing to give fifty. It was dragging on for a long time. Maya knew the boys were having more fun, just by watching the girls beg.

Maya made a last offer. "We will let the groom have one shoe of his choice for fifty rupees, and he can hop all the way home on one foot!" The whole group of girls started chuckling and cackling at Maya's clever idea.

Suraj was watching the spectacle from a distance, making mental notes on what to expect if he were to get married. He was impressed with the way in which the girls made the groom cough up the money. The groom's mother ended the game by giving all the girls silver rings to honor the tradition.

Soon came the moment for the doli, the beautifully decorated, carved-wood enclosure with velvet and satin upholstery and curtains. The bride would sit in the doli as her brothers carried her to her new husband's home. The departure of the bride was the most touching ceremony Suraj had ever seen. Perhaps it was Maya's emotional response that disturbed him as she tearfully said good-bye to her cousin.

Maya realized that now, her cousin officially belonged to her husband and her new family. She watched as the bride said good-bye to her other loved ones, glanced back at the house, and got in the doli. *The biggest change in her life is about to take place*, Maya thought. *She's expected to accept her husband's family as her own. The thought of living away from her own parents must be very scary to her.* Everyone present from both sides shed a few tears. Maya and her cousin had shared dreams of having a wonderful husband and loving in-laws. Maya hoped that her cousin's dreams would come true. She prayed in her heart and wished her cousin a happy life, even as she realized that she, too, would have to leave her loved ones one day.

Maya felt someone grab her hand from behind as the

doli was leaving. She turned around and saw Suraj right behind her. Like a blushing bride, she took the corner of her dupputta (her veil) in her teeth to hide her smile. Then she twisted her wrist to get free before anyone spotted Suraj holding her arm.

Suraj let go of her—he knew it wasn't proper for an unmarried girl to be with a man. He pointed toward the barn and whispered, "Meet me there."

It was getting dark and the remaining guests were saying good-bye to each other. It had been exhausting day for all. The rich food and plenty of fun activities had tired everyone, and most of the family members and guests already had gone to bed. It had gone quiet all of sudden; Belan and Shanti had also left to go home, assuming that Suraj would stay behind to help the family with putting the place back together. The marquee and pergolas needed to be taken down, chairs and tables were to be placed in the trucks, and borrowed cots and bedding was to be returned. There was a lot of work to be done yet.

Suraj waited for quite some time in the barn, but Maya did not show up. He initially assumed that she had been called up by an aunt or grandmother who kept her away. The thought of rejection never occurred to him. He was very sure from their first meeting that the flame was burning at both ends. Their body language, eye contact, and other signals were enough for him to know that she liked him too. No words were needed to communicate. He sat on an upside-down bucket near the neatly packed haystack but then realized how ludicrous he would look to anyone who saw him. The thought that someone might question his purpose in the barn crossed his mind, so he got up to leave. As he did, he heard faint tinkle of an anklet. He prayed it was Maya's.

And there she was—a girl luminous with beauty—in front of him like a dream. He held both of her hands in his own as she began to explain, but he didn't care what had taken her so long. It only mattered that she was there. He had fallen madly in love with her. All he wanted to ask her was if she would marry him. He looked in her eyes and blurted out, "Will you be my wife?"

Maya blushed. She was glad that it was dark in the barn—she didn't want to be seen secretly talking to a man. She'd put her reputation in jeopardy by meeting him, knowing that a small misunderstanding or rumor could have put her and her family in a very awkward situation, especially as her family were guests at her cousin's house.

Suraj told Maya about being in the military and that he intended to continue his career in army. "I don't want you to have false hopes or expectations," he explained. "It would be wrong for me to assume that you would agree to such arrangement. I have seen my mother in such a wife's role, and I recognized her devotion for my father in his absence. Women don't have very many choices, but I don't want to keep my future wife in dark about certain truths in life."

Maya nodded demurely. "I am familiar with your family's needs." The reality was that she was too young and naïve to know the real meaning of marriage, relationships, or intimacy, but she knew that every girl had to get married and do her duty to her husband and his family. It was purely from her sense of duty and what she knew she was expected to do that helped her answer Suraj. "I am ready to take on the role as your wife."

Beauty, innocence, and good nature were sought-after traits in any bride for any respectable man. Maya possessed all these qualities and much more. She was fun to be with and had a great sense of humor and wit, yet she was a simple, humble girl who valued integrity, honesty, and kindness above all. Suraj found her not only mentally and emotionally compatible but extremely attractive. He loved her easygoing ways. Her innocent, gullible nature excited him. All of sudden, Suraj had an aching desire to kiss her. A pang shot through him, and he was fascinated by how her lips quivered when she talked. Her scent was so intoxicating that as an honorable man, he fought the urge to hold her and kiss her right there.

Maya walked backward away from him, her steps nimble but sure, portraying her willpower. Her pearly white teeth and her beautiful smile were driving Suraj insane. Maya could sense the effect she had on him. Although she was a young girl of eighteen, she had made a mark on his heart.

Suraj was completely lost for words. Nothing was said between the two, yet unspoken words were understood. He still waited for a signal, a nod from Maya to confirm her approval. He knew Maya was too young and a little hesitant. He pulled on Maya's finger as he held her hand again, hoping for a response that indicated she felt the same about him as he felt for her.

She looked right in his eyes and said, "It took a lot of courage for a girl like me to meet you here. I risked my family's good name and reputation for you. That should tell you something."

He simply nodded and admired her honesty. Before he released her hand, he said, "I am sorry for causing you any trouble."

Maya responded, "You are worth the trouble," and with that, she ran toward the house, leaving Suraj with a huge grin on his face. Suraj wasn't surprised that his mother had liked her.

A month later, Suraj left for his duty, and there was a simple ceremony, where Suraj's parents visited Maya's home and performed an engagement ceremony. It was a common practice for the groom's family to visit the bride's family to initiate the beginnings of wedding ceremonies. Maya's village was just a few miles away. A mutual relative had arranged and accompanied them on their visit. A head priest of a temple fixed an auspicious day for the ceremony, which was announced prior to their visit. The family's elders gave their blessings and an exchange of gifts and jewelry.

Maya was very subdued on her engagement, as she didn't realize the significance of this ritual until an elder relative explained it to her by saying, "You are going to enter the next stage of your life." Maya had known many girls who had gotten married in her village, left home, and started a new family. She imagined she would do the same but not quite so soon; that day still seemed a million miles away. The thought of becoming

Suraj's wife, having an intimate relationship, and living in a different home with a different family was very unnerving. Growing up at home, surrounded by her mother, father, and four brothers and their wives was all she knew.

Having lots of girlfriends was not considered a good trait for a daughter. Mothers kept their young girls busy at home with different chores after school. Maya was always busy with an embroidery project, knitting, or sewing. She was a great help to her sisters-in-law and in return, they all spoiled her a bit. Her brothers were very protective of her, and they allowed her to get away with a lot. Going with her sisters-in-law to towns and cities, unlike other girls her age, made her the envy of other village girls. She developed a great sense of fashion, as well as the hobby of reading poems. She became the one from whom others asked advice for clothes and hair. Her own interest in poetry kept her busy and entertained. Maya was so beloved in her village that when people heard the news of her wedding, they were crushed and happy at the same time—they would miss her.

To leave the maiden life behind and start a new life was proving to be a daunting task for Maya. It suddenly seemed to be happening so fast—she had bumped into Suraj at her cousin's wedding and now, so suddenly, it was only matter of months before she would get married. She was saddened by the knowledge that she would take only memories of her old life to the new home.

Maya's sisters-in-law reminded her that she should consider herself lucky. "The man you are going to marry is not only someone who expressed his love to you but someone to whom you are very attracted," one said,

"Suraj is a handsome, charming young soldier who is going to keep you very happy," said another. "He is of sound character—a gentleman who is kind and considerate and knows how to take care of his family."

Suraj's reputation among the villagers was of a gentle and hardworking man who didn't shirk away from dirty field work or from lending a hand to a neighbor. He was genuinely sincere and thoughtful. The emotional support he gave his mother when she lost her older son showed his true character. Everybody in the village had very high regard for Suraj and his family. Maya felt proud and honored to be part of Suraj's family.

As the wedding date neared, Maya needed her mother's reassurances from time to time. She had witnessed the separation her sisters-in-law had experienced when they joined the family, but they were fortunate to have her adoring mother as their mother-in-law to embrace them and support them. Shanti could never replace her mother, but Maya really liked her. She had found her to be a warm, caring, and very wise woman. *She will be a good mother-in-law*, Maya told herself. Maya was well aware of the tragedy that occurred in her future in-laws' family, and she had respected their sentiments. Being a young girl, she was full of compassion and empathy for people who were robbed of their loved ones in tragic circumstances.

1928 — India

MAYA AND SURAJ'S WEDDING

There was a mixed atmosphere of jubilation and anguish. The family decided on a quiet ceremony, with the consent of Maya's family. Maya had her hands and feet covered in henna, the most beautiful, intricate design she had seen on any girl's hands ever. Her youngest sister-in-law had spent hours in creating an amazing design. She had promised Maya that she would give her the best henna design on her wedding.

Every year, when married women applied henna on their hands and feet, Maya would beg her sisters-in-law to do it for her, but she hadn't been allowed to apply henna as yet. Now, on the night before her wedding, all the village ladies were present at the henna ceremony, which was followed by more dancing and singing. Passersby could hear bursts of laughter.

Maya's mother made sure that Maya had an early night. She needed rest for next day's ceremonies. Her eldest sister-in-law led her to her room, made her change into comfortable night clothes, and helped her into bed. The henna on her hands was almost dried, but Maya wasn't supposed to wash until the next morning. Her sister-in-law turned off the oil lamps and wished Maya good night. Just as she was leaving, Maya asked her sister-in-law to sit with her for few minutes—she was like Maya's second mother, as Maya spent the most time with her.

Maya pointed toward her pillow. "My henna might not be quite dry. Would you reach under my pillow and take out what is there?"

Her sister-in-law pulled a wrapped present from under the pillow and opened it. It contained a couple of Maya's unused notebooks, some poems she had written, and pencils. There also was a note that read: "Please don't give up on reading. Practice every day." Her sister-in-law had been totally illiterate. Maya had been trying to teach her how to read and write for years. Now, she kissed Maya on her forehead and promised that she would try, even though the kitchen, babies, and other household duties always came before her study session.

As her sister-in-law left the room, Maya noticed that the high-pitched voices and the sounds from the small, barrel-shaped drum known as the dholki, which had been part of the festivities, had subsided. It felt as if the entire universe had gone to sleep. The night was so still and serene, as if conserving energy for the very special occasion the next day. It was a pleasant night, with a light cool breeze. There was not a single cloud in the moonlit sky, and stars were twinkling. Maya's eyes were wide open, watching the elements of nature through the open window of her room. Her grandma was snoring away like a train in the bed next to her. She was about to turn away from the window in an attempt to fall asleep when she saw a shadow.

Her heart fluttered, and she held her breath until she heard a whisper. She raised herself on her elbows and tried to look outside the window. It was her cousin, who was visiting her for the wedding. Maya could barely hear her, let alone understand what she was saying. Her voice was hoarse, as the nonstop chattering, singing, and screaming with joy at the henna evening had left lot of girls' throats dry and sore.

Maya went to the window and saw her cousin take an envelope from under her shawl. "Take this," she hissed, handing it to Maya—she didn't sound happy about being up in the middle of the night. Maya took the envelope from her and thanked her. She ripped the envelope open without caring about her henna. It was a note from Suraj and something else in a little package. She looked around to see if grandmother was still asleep and tried to focus her eyes to read the note in the dim moonlight.

The note read: "To my dearest love, I write this to you with my heart in my hand. You gave my heart a leap the day I watched you dance at your cousin's wedding. Your smile took my breath away. I never knew such happiness ever existed. With every breath I take, I vow to love you and honor you until eternity. Please wear the toe ring I've enclosed. I wait in anticipation of seeing you as my bride tomorrow. Sweet dreams!"

Maya felt an electric shock go through her body. She

held the toe ring and slipped the silver band on her middle toe. She put the note under her pillow and then dreamed sweet dreams.

The next morning, Maya was almost ready when the baraat reached the gate. Her mother used toasted red chilies and made an invisible halo around Maya's head for protection from the evil eye. Maya looked radiant in her red lehenga (bridal skirt). She was loaded with gold jewelry; her red bangles covered her forearms. Her veil covered half of her beautiful face, showing only her lips, chin, and neck. Her eyes were downcast, with her head slightly bowed. She looked strikingly beautiful.

Suraj, too, was all decked out in a silk Sherwani—the groom's wedding outfit—with a long pearl necklace. His face was covered by a veil known as a Sehra, which was made out of strings of pearls.

Maya saw her Prince Charming riding on a white horse through the open window. His family and friends who had come to join his wedding ceremony were dancing in a procession, with loud music playing through the loud speakers carried by band wallas.

Every ritual was completed without a hiccup. All the guests present wished the couple a happy life. Finally, it was time for the doli. Maya's sisters-in-law were bit concerned about Maya since she did not eat much all day. Maya had lost her appetite, because she was overwhelmed and nervous. With teary eyes and a lump in her throat, she called for her mother, as the doli time drew closer. It was matter of minutes before Maya would say good-bye to her family. Her mother wanted to take a moment to be with her daughter. All she could say was, "I do not need to give advice to my sensible daughter. You have been an obedient daughter, and I'm sure you'll make us proud in the future too. Your father and I will miss you very much. These doors will always be open for you. I hope and pray that your new family appreciates you and never lets you feel lonely." She blessed her daughter, as tears rolled down her cheeks, and she walked her out for the doli ceremony.

Maya's sisters-in-law delicately led her mother away from Maya and straightened Maya's veil. Maya said good-bye to everyone. Her father and brothers were in a trance; separation anxiety was taking its toll on everyone. At that point, Shanti came forward and gently wiped her tears. She looked in Maya's eyes, hoping to connect with her heart so that she might understand that every girl has to endure this painful separation.

Maya had no idea that Suraj had walked away from the scene. He blamed himself for the hurt it caused Maya. He felt guilty, as if he was stealing her from her parents.

All through the journey, Maya sobbed quietly. By the time they reached home, Maya was exhausted. Belan, Suraj, and Shanti had arranged a warm welcome for Maya. All sorts of rituals were performed by ladies in the village. An element of excitement in seeing the new bride was present in the air. Suraj and Maya entered the threshold together. Their mother poured oil on each side of the threshold as a good omen. Then she held a small pot of milk, encircled the couple's heads, and took small sips of milk herself. She repeated this five times—this was to bless the bride with sons and daughters. Daughters-in-law were considered to be Lakshmi, the goddess of wealth, as a new bride was known to bring good fortune. Other rituals and games, such as finding pennies in milky water or untying each other's knotted bracelets, were simply to break the ice and as an opportunity for the couple to touch each other. It was all to lighten the atmosphere. Shanti made sure that Maya and Suraj had their meal together before they were sent to their bridal chamber.

Suraj walked in his room to find Maya sitting very still on his bed with her wedding outfit still on. Her veil covered her face. The sight of her brought a smile to his face. Maya was exhausted but could not close her eyes to rest. The large room had two carved wooden wardrobes against one of the walls, a huge bed, and two chairs and a desk in a corner; it felt very cold and intimidating to Maya. Suraj closed the door behind him and put the door latch on in one easy motion. Maya jumped out of her skin when she heard the door latch.

"Do you need company?" Suraj teasingly asked her as he approached the bed. Maya stayed very still behind her veil. He gently lifted her veil and held her beautiful face in his hands. He was admiring his beautiful wife, but she shied away as he placed his forefinger under her chin and tilted her head so that he could feast his eyes on her face. In the dim light of the oil lamps, Maya's eyes remained downcast while Suraj kissed her on her lips. She let out a moan and pulled away. Maya was so shy and nervous that she hid her face in the veil again, and Suraj walked away from the bed with a big grin.

"I'm going to change into my night clothes," he said. "Are you going to bed all decked up like that?" After removing his shoes, he took off his clothes and hung them neatly on the hooks. He pulled a fresh kurta—a long cotton shirt—from the wardrobe and slipped it on. In two long strides he reached the drinks cabinet and poured himself a brandy. "Would you like to have a little drink too?" he asked, glancing over his shoulder at her. Most men considered it immoral for women to consume a drink or two, but his mother and grandmother both enjoyed occasional drinks. Suraj was aware of Maya's emotional and mental state, and he just wanted her to relax a little. He needed to relax as well, to absorb all of what had happened during the day. Realizing he was married to the woman he loved made him feel blessed by the gods. His desire to fulfill Maya's every need, to make her forget the pain of leaving her parents' home, and to make passionate love to her was overwhelming. He knew it was different for girls, that it was not enjoyable if she wasn't ready. Maya was clearly very nervous and tense—she had curled up in a tight ball, clutching her knees with crossed arms. He sat down on the bed next to her. "May I hold your hands?" he asked. "Don't be frightened." He wanted her to know he wasn't someone who would pounce on her and ravish her.

She lowered her arms, allowing him to hold her hands, and though she still turned her face away, she felt him slip a ring on her finger. Maya spun around to face him as he kissed her hand. He whispered, "A little gesture to show you that I will always love you, as long as I live."

On the second attempt to unveil his bride, their eyes locked on one another. Suraj's face lit up in love. The glow on his face in the dim light of a lamp made him look so handsome, and his puppy eyes were full of love for his wife. Maya lowered her eyes; her long eyelashes were like a black curtain on her soft, fair skin. Suraj felt a jolt in his groin as he spoke ever so softly, telling Maya that she was the most beautiful girl he had ever seen. Maya quivered as he kissed her forehead, her cheeks, her nose, her chin, and then lips again. Maya didn't push him away this time. She was absolutely still, with her eyes closed.

Suraj was intoxicated with her scent and kept breathing into her neck, kissing her all over. All of a sudden, he stopped and decided to help Maya take off her wedding outfit. Her gold jewelry was distracting him. He slid down the bed and poured Maya a fresh glass of water—she needed the drink badly as she was gasping for air, and her mouth was very dry. She drank half the glass and gave it back to Suraj. Finishing the rest in one gulp, he filled the glass again and handed to Maya. Maya declined, and Suraj ingeniously knocked the glass and spilled the water all over Maya. She jumped as the cold water seeped through her blouse. Suraj apologized, swept her off the bed in his strong arms, and placed her on the floor. In the commotion, Maya's veil came off. Suraj picked it up and hung it on the back of the chair. He apologized again for being clumsy. Maya sensed foul play, for she knew it was a deliberate act. She secretly smiled as Suraj grabbed a towel and started patting Maya down on her front. She turned away from him to hide her shyness, as Suraj held her close from behind, not letting her get away.

He removed her earrings and gently bit on her earlobe, sending shivers down her spine. He untied her necklace, which was like a gold armor, and dropped it off in the tray on the table. Next, he slipped Maya's bangles off her slim hands and let them fall on the floor, making delicious musical sounds. All the while, he was holding Maya tightly in his arms, kissing the back of her neck. She tried to wiggle free as Suraj unhooked her blouse from the back. Maya turned to face him but hid her face in his chest. He tugged at the knot of her lehenga tassel, and it came undone and landed on the floor. She tried to cover her nakedness with her hands, but Suraj was far too quick. In one smooth move, he lifted her off the floor and placed her on the bed. At a jaguar's speed, he was out of his clothes and landed conveniently next to her. The scent of jasmine in Maya's hair was driving him insane. He wanted to make love to her but didn't feel right to force her against her wishes. He repeatedly told her that he wouldn't hurt her. Maya stopped struggling. She believed him. She knew she would have to give in, as Suraj had a right to her body. He was surprised when Maya asked for a brandy. Suraj ran to the cupboard, took two glasses out, and poured a small amount in each. Maya grabbed a bed sheet around her as she sat up to accept her drink. Suraj expected Maya to knock the drink down in one gulp, but the strong smell of brandy knocked the wind out of her. She held on to the glass for several minutes but didn't have the courage to swallow it. Every time she brought the glass closer to her mouth to take a sip, the vile smell of alcohol put her off. After several attempts, Suraj grabbed the drink from her, pinched her nose, and poured the drink down her throat. She tried to spit it out, but it was all gone inside of her. Amused and entertained, Suraj patted her shoulder and said, "See? It wasn't difficult. Now here is something I want you to try—I am sure you will start to like it." He turned off the lamps and made sweet love to his wife. She had lot to learn, but Suraj was a patient teacher.

The next day as the family was waking, there was a loud knock on their front gate. Tejan and his son Mangal, who hadn't been invited to the wedding, were at the gate. The house servant ran to inform Belan and to ask permission to allow them in. Belan sent him to fetch his mother and wife and walked toward the gate himself. He greeted his brother and nephew with respect and brought them in the courtyard. By then, Shanti and her mother-in-law had joined them. Shanti sent for tea and breakfast. She observed that Tejan was wounded by the fact that he had not been invited to the wedding.

His pensive mood seemed bizarre to Belan, He had expected Tejan to be angry and abusive toward him for the slight. Before Belan could say anything, their mother spoke up on her son's behalf. "It was my decision that only immediate family be part of the wedding," she said. "And remember your past actions—that also led to the decision."

Tejan could not take the insults and was about to leave when, surprisingly, Mangal, who was watching for Suraj and his new bride, said, "Let's not leave just yet, Father. We should wait and bless the newlyweds first."

Grandma sensed bad intentions. "No, you should go," she insisted. "They are not awake yet." Belan tried to intervene, but his mother insisted that they leave. Belan stepped aside and let his brother and nephew leave.

After they left, Belan's mother warned, "If you ever trust your snake of a brother, you will be the biggest fool. You must promise that even after my death, you will not trust him." The wise old woman was trying to protect Suraj's new bride from the vultures. She didn't trust Mangal's intentions.

Suraj and Maya were getting to know one another. Shanti introduced the new bride to her neighbors and relatives in the village. Maya was always polite and courteous toward everyone. She was surprised by how soon she got used to the new environment. The first few days flew by so fast, and waking up in her husband's arms and fixing his breakfast was pure joy. To have regular visitors bless them with happy marriage throughout the week kept her so occupied that she forgot about her own family.

A few weeks later, as it was time for Suraj to leave for work, Maya grew quiet and withdrawn. "I'm in the same predicament as you are," Suraj admitted. "It is very hard for me to leave you. I've gotten used to you and have started depending on you a lot for little things. The thought of you tagging along as I move from post to post doesn't make any sense. You wouldn't feel comfortable among strangers."

The thought of Suraj going away frightened Maya, but the thought of living alone in the officers' quarters paralyzed her. Maya had formed a bond with Shanti and Grandmother. She spent the mornings with her mother-in-law, learning about the household chores. She was getting to know people around the village. Shanti never had a bad word to say about anyone, and she didn't influence Maya with her opinion. She wanted young Maya to learn from her own experiences, form her own opinions, and make judgments according to the circumstances.

Maya also spent lot of time with Grandmother, whom she admired a lot. She was very impressed with old lady's sharp wit and directness. Her strong opinions about certain issues and her assertive nature toward the servants came across as cold and mean, but in reality, she was being cruel to be kind. She didn't believe in giving anyone anything until it was earned. Maya was like a sponge that absorbed the kind and the harsh lessons from both women.

Maya had been married just over a year when she woke up to learn that their beloved grandmother had passed away in her sleep. Maya sent an urgent telegram, informing Suraj of Grandmother's death. Belan sent a message to his brother, informing him of funeral services. Tejan sent a message back: "I am glad the witch is gone." His despicable message was cruel and hurtful. It pierced Belan's heart to learn that his brother was so hateful. It frightened him a little that if his brother harbored such ugly feelings for his own mother, how could he trust his loyalty toward Belan and his family?

1932

SURAJ AND PETER IN SERVICE
OF THE INDIAN ARMY

*S*uraj had joined the Training Battalion of the Punjab Regiment in Delhi right after his matriculation, receiving a salary of fifteen rupees per month. He was considered an excellent cadet. He excelled at his training and impressed his superiors with his focused and sharp mind. He graduated two terms early from the academy. It was wonderful news for his proud parents. Shanti had celebrated her son's success by sharing sweets with the whole village.

After completing his training in 1925, Suraj was selected for training as a prospective candidate for the Indian Military Academy at Dehradun. The fear of another world war loomed like a dark cloud. That put all cadets on intensive training. Later, Suraj was posted to the 1st Battalion of Punjab Regiment, which was called Sher Dil Paltan, or Brave Soldier, based at Lahore, in the same barracks where he had been a sepoy. His battalion moved from Lahore to Secunderabad in 1930—that's where he met Captain Peter McPhee, his senior recruiting officer and a trainer to new recruits.

Peter appeared to be a noble officer who demanded great discipline from his fellow soldiers. He believed consistency and routine were the key factors for the physical fitness of a soldier. He jogged every morning, rain or shine. Suraj, also an athlete, accompanied Peter. They created a running team with fellow soldiers and competed against one another. The respected teams trained together, and on Sunday, they played cricket. The friendly game eventually became so popular that their wives and many others came to watch it. The whole afternoon turned into an event where ladies laid out picnic baskets on the blankets near the field, and gentlemen dressed in white shirts and slacks to hit the ball with the bat. The friendly game brought Peter and Suraj closer, and they respected each other's opinions without discussing sensitive issues. Both learned new things about the other's culture as the world was changing in front of them.

Some white officers didn't approve of Peter's friendship with Suraj, but Peter didn't take any notice of such criticism. He never indulged in talks with fellow officers when they made derogatory remarks about the locals. He kept a low profile at the social gatherings and remained neutral when officers got in heated debates about the new revolutionaries causing trouble for the British. Peter had not realized the extent of the cruelty, injustice, and discrimination by the British government, and it was hard for him to absorb and ignore some of the wrongs within society. He loathed the English for referring to themselves as higher gentry and a civilized society versus the illiterate, poor, and dirty Indians. It was embarrassing for Peter to see that British kept the Indians at arm's length, looked down upon them, and didn't allow the locals near their women or children when they visited.

Signs were posted at certain white areas that read: "Indians and dogs not allowed." Peter was horrified and ashamed by that. As Peter spent more time in India, living among Indian fellow soldiers, he grew to understand their ways and culture. He realized that the Indian civilization was far superior to colonized England. The British not only negated the Indian culture, but they introduced alien education to cut off the Indians from their traditional heritage and cultural pride. They encouraged the rich middle class to go to England to be educated in a "civilized" country, which gained economic power through enslaving others. *How ironic is that?* Peter asked himself.

It was during the peaceful times that Suraj visited home regularly, pampered his wife with gifts, and took her out on visits to the town. He was a father to two beautiful little girls, Bani and Geet. They were born just one year apart. Maya was taking care of the children as well as taking care of her in-laws, but Suraj thought she'd seemed restless during his last visit. But he recalled how desperately she had wanted him to make love to her. Bold and beautiful Maya enticed and seduced her husband at odd places and at odd times. At first, Suraj thought of her ideas were inappropriate, but soon he was bewitched by Maya's spell and followed her from the rooftop to the cornfield to the barn. He found Maya extremely sexy and beautiful. Her voluptuousness, her bossiness, and playfully controlling nature excited him.

She had expressed her wish to have a son, and her need to get pregnant on Suraj's every visit was so intense that he felt exhausted. He tried to console her by telling her that he valued their daughters as much as he would value a son. He wondered if she felt pressured by his mother, although he doubted that very much. Suraj made love to her every day on his short visit to compensate for the physical distance they had in their marriage.

Suraj discussed his job prospects and transfers with Maya, informing her of his whereabouts. He talked about the general feeling of the Indian army with regard to his father, who was also very concerned about various riots and uprisings all over India. On the last day of Suraj's visit, Maya embraced her husband tightly as he held her face and kissed her on her mouth. Her face was wet from tears, and Suraj felt terrible—he felt as if he had cheated her of her happiness. He lifted both of his daughters in his arms, kissed them good-bye, and promised to buy them dolls on his next visit. He felt torn between his family and his country.

1936

ATTACK ON PETER

Back in the army barracks, Suraj took a keen interest in reading English newspapers to learn of the English economy and the mood of the English public. He was trying to comprehend the economics of his own country and found it hard to believe that the resources and wealth generated from Indian industry was astronomical. Europe had nothing to export that was in demand in India, whereas the British Empire earned most of its wealth from imports of cotton and silk goods, which faced duties of 70 to 80 percent, as compared to British imports duties of 2 to 4 percent. This drain of funds from India to the UK was one of the major controversial issues between Indian nationals and defenders of the British Raj. Daily news in the papers left no doubt in people's minds that if these funds had been invested in India, they could have made a significant contribution to raising income levels.

Atrocities were committed by the British with their

usual cunning and calculative conspiracy. Farmers were forced to switch from subsistence farming to commercial crops, such as opium, jute, tea, and coffee. That resulted in famine, and it enraged the Indian farmers. Another issue of Indian nationals was that India had to pay for its 300,000 citizens in uniform, as well as for the highly paid white British officers in the form of inflated taxes for Indian peasants. Suraj was flabbergasted by the cunning scheme as he discussed this with other Indian soldiers. British politicians defended and justified the position by offering provisions of railways and postal and telegram services to enrich the nation. That was needed to put the economy back on its track, but Suraj wondered, *For whose benefit?*

Suraj, Peter, and many others like them were slowly waking up to in the truth, and in England, the general public and the opposition party also shamed and criticized the British government of wrongdoing. Suraj decided that Indians were totally perplexed by the British plots. What the British did not realize was that India had a far longer history of civilization than Britain had. The problem Suraj saw was that India's civilization was cloaked in dhotis, saris, and turbans, as well as a few ancient barbaric practices, such as the terrible caste system and the sati practice, in which a widow was forced to throw herself on her dead husband's funeral pyre.

Suraj argued that what the British were doing was equally barbaric. They had robbed and enslaved not just a few people but an entire country. Peter admitted that Britain was not too far removed from equally medieval practices. Strange-looking wigs worn by judges and robes worn by priests were equally medieval. It was such a shame that people in shirts, skirts, and trousers who came to India were convinced that India was uncivilized. "It's about time," Peter argued, "that the world recognizes that every culture and every country has a dark side, but why does the developed world see the evils of other countries but not their own?"

It was 1936, when Annie followed Peter for the third time on his posting—first to Dehradun and Delhi and now Lahore. The army base had the biggest artillery camp. Peter was in charge of his unit—thirty-six soldiers and two officers. Annie was pleasantly surprised by the accommodations and the travel arrangements Peter had made for her—a comfortable journey on the train and a great welcome by Peter's orderly, Seva Singh, who had freshly made ice tea waiting on the tray. When she arrived, however, Annie was looking only for the bathroom—the bathroom project was always the top priority. Annie took a tour of the bungalow and made mental notes of what needed to be done. She was tired from the journey and took a nap in the hammock under the banyan tree in the backyard. A little kitten was curled up at her feet when she woke up. Kittens and small dogs often found a friend in Annie. She named the kitten Magic and gave her some milk from the kitchen.

Suraj was waiting for her on the veranda of their living quarters the next morning when Annie woke up. The housemaid had set up the morning tea and a light breakfast for two on the table. Annie had met Suraj a few times through Peter, as they were close friends in the same unit. Annie's face lit up on seeing Suraj; she had not forgotten the fun evenings spent together, laughing and eating. How Peter and Suraj made fun of Annie when they showed her how to eat a ripe mango out of its skin. Annie loved the mango chutney that Maya sent for Suraj, which he shared with Peter and Annie. She had gone through the entire contents of the jar in just a couple of days and had licked her fingers clean. Peter was away on assignment but had instructed his servants to take care of the work and any help Annie needed. Annie was touched by the hospitality and simplicity of Seva Singh, who was courteous and eager to help. Peter was very well respected and loved by his Indian troops.

Suraj had brought her the message from Peter's lieutenant general that Peter was ordered to attend to an urgent situation. "They expect it to be resolved in a couple of days," Suraj said. "In the meantime, if you need any assistance, notify the unit commander immediately."

Annie totally understood the importance of Peter's duty. She was glad that Suraj was there to keep her the company. He had just returned back from his village after seeing his wife and children. Annie didn't feel like meeting the other army wives on her first day in town. She wanted to wait for her husband to do the introductions. Seva Singh and his wife, Rani, lived in the separate barracks away from the army residential camp.

Suraj left after tea and promised to check back with her in the afternoon. At lunchtime, Seva offered to bring food from the mess hall, but Annie didn't care for the food. She grabbed an apple and settled in the hammock to read her book. She fell asleep and didn't wake until Suraj returned, and by then she was starving.

Suraj felt responsible for entertaining her. "I have a plan for the evening," he announced. "I don't think it's a good idea for you to stay indoors, waiting for Peter. I'd like to take you to see a Nautanki—that's an Indian folk opera."

While Annie changed into fresh clothes, Suraj got his bicycle from his barracks. Annie sat on the back of his bike, holding Suraj around his waist, as he took her for a short ride to the village center, where the Nautanki was to be performed. It was getting dark by this time, and the place was filling up fast with local men, women, and children. Suraj took Annie by her arm and led her through the crowd. The Nautanki was the biggest entertainment medium in the villages. Its rich musical compositions and humorous entertainment made Annie forget Peter for the rest of the evening. Suraj translated the Nautanki for Annie—it was more like a Punch and Judy show—and Annie had stomach cramps from laughing so hard.

The next day, Annie didn't hear from Suraj or Peter's superiors all day. She finally asked Peter's senior officers about him that evening at the mess hall. She was asked to call the office for more news in the morning. When she asked about Suraj, she was told that he was sent to check up on the same situation where Peter had gone. None of the soldiers had returned yet.

Annie had trouble sleeping that night. Niggling worry

had started crawling in her head. She was beginning to see the real danger of rebellious riots. Peter had mentioned his concerns lately. *Is Peter in danger?* she wondered. She stayed up and tried to read a little. She wished Mary was there and thought of calling her, but then she didn't want to worry her unnecessarily. Still, being alone at a time like this was petrifying.

Seva brought breakfast from the hall mess the next morning, and Annie quickly washed herself and got ready. She glanced over the news on the front page of yesterday's newspaper. Nothing important deserved her attention except a picture of two young women. They were holding handguns and had bandanas on their heads. The photo gave Annie the chills. She read the article while she ate her breakfast. It covered the news of Surya Sen, who led the most active Chittagong group. He had actively participated in the non-cooperation movement and was arrested and imprisoned for two years for the revolutionary activity of capturing two police armories in Chittagong. They'd hoisted the national flag amid shouts of "Bande Mataram and Inquilab Zindabad!" (Gratitude to Mother India! Long live the revolution!) After a fierce fight, in which over eighty British troops and twelve revolutionaries died, Surya Sen was caught and arrested. Last week, he'd been hanged.

The women in the picture were campaigning to avenge his death. Annie was shocked at the hatred in their eyes. She threw the paper back on the table and rushed out to meet the commanding officer to learn of her husband's whereabouts.

Suraj had been sent with his entire unit and a second officer to the troubled spot. The team was well equipped with weapons when they reached a small town. He soon learned that Peter's unit had been attacked. Peter and his team were there for delivery of artillery, as they'd been instructed. Notorious gang members received the information and attacked Peter's men. Peter was missing, and half of the men were terribly injured and burned from numerous grenades and gunpowder blasts.

Suraj investigated the entire village for Peter's whereabouts, but there was no sign of him. Soldiers described the gang but were unable to identify them, as they had covered their faces with dark masks and rode on horseback in the middle of the night. The attack was well planned and executed ferociously and suddenly.

Suraj returned back to headquarters to report his findings and then decided to stop by to see Annie.

Annie jumped when she heard his knock on the door. She ran to open it and flung her arms around Suraj. She couldn't look in his face—she was afraid he had bad news.

"No news is good news," Suraj told her. "That's all I can say at this point."

"Please, Suraj, take me to Peter!" she begged, distraught and hysterical.

Suraj could tell she'd been crying—her eyes were red and puffy. "You need to rest," he told her. "Forgive me, but you look as if you haven't slept."

Annie dissolved in tears again, and Suraj didn't know how to console her. "I'm worried about Peter, too," he admitted as he poured her a neat gin and made her drink it. He stayed with Annie until very late, just sitting quietly, and finally she fell asleep on the sofa. Suraj covered her with a light blanket and walked out of the bungalow.

A search party with guard dogs was sent in all directions near where the attack had taken place. All unit soldiers were interviewed by senior officers. They knew that Peter couldn't have just vanished into thin air. He'd either been kidnapped—or killed. The senior officers' wives and the female staff tried to give Annie the emotional support she needed, but Annie was falling apart. She sent telegrams to Mary and to Peter's parents. The army officially listed Peter as missing in action, but the search for him continued. Suraj vowed that he would hunt down the people who have abducted Peter. Annie trusted him completely and was grateful that her husband's friend was there for her. She thanked Suraj for being her friend and protector.

Days went by, and there was no news of Peter McPhee. His senior officers were baffled by his disappearance and felt ashamed that they could not do more. Peter was one of the favorite officers of his unit, even though it was true that some of Peter's peers didn't approve of his close friendship with Suraj. Everyone in Peter's unit was under suspicion, including Suraj.

Posters with Peter's photo were posted all over the towns and neighboring villages. The British army was investigating it as a kidnapping case, although no party had come forward or taken responsibility of this action.

Suraj was terribly affected by the loss of his dear

friend. He couldn't concentrate on his work, and his colleagues noticed how irritable he had become. Suraj requested a leave of absence so he could investigate Peter's disappearance on his own. He met with various types of people and talked to people he normally would not have approached. He noticed people and studied them. It was amazing insight for Suraj—the experience of hearing other people's stories, their daily banter in life, and their simple pleasures. Army officers generally were cocooned in their own world, but now, Suraj was learning life's tough lessons on the streets of Lahore.

Over the days that Suraj searched for Peter, he grew tired and weary and almost was on the verge of giving up. Then on the afternoon of his tenth day, as he sat at a tea stall having a cup of tea in a remote village by the river, Suraj noticed a strange-looking man with dark kohl around his eyes. His dramatic appearance drew Suraj's attention. The man had a small package with him that he carried under his arm. He ordered the tea and squatted on his haunches, waiting patiently. He didn't make eye contact with anyone, and no one seemed to be bothered by him. Suraj thought of him simply as a traveler passing through the village.

The village bus arrived at the bus stop, and there was great commotion as people ran toward it to get on board. The strange-looking man seemed in a great hurry, and as he ran toward the bus, he left his package on the ground where he'd been sitting. Suraj noticed the package, but by that time, the bus had left with the stranger on it. Suraj picked up the package, just curious to see what the man had been carrying but then left behind. Suraj opened the package and was confused when he found a pair of pants and couple of shirts. The man had been wearing the very traditional dhoti, the loose fabric that men wore around their waists, so the pants and shirts seemed out of place. The clothes in the package also seemed too large for the small man. Alarm bells started ringing in Suraj's head, but now, how could he find the man? He ran to the people at the bus stand to see if anyone knew where the bus was headed. Three or four people spoke at once with different answers. Suraj took a long breath and thought hard. *I have a feeling that strange man will return for his clothes*, he told himself.

A few minutes later, Suraj saw the man running toward the tea stall, totally out of breath. Suraj imagined him hollering at the driver to stop the bus. *He must have run all the way back*, Suraj thought, discreetly placing the package back where he'd found it. The strange-looking man seemed relieved to see his package.

Suraj's instincts told him to follow the man. He waited patiently for the man to board the next overflowing bus. Then Suraj got on and positioned himself where he could keep his eye on the man. When the man got off the bus, Suraj got off too and followed him to a part of town where soft music was playing and the sweet smell of jasmine was in the air. By then, it was completely dark, the only light coming from the lanterns that lit the entrances of some homes. Suraj saw the man enter in one of the courtyards and knock on the door of a large house. A woman in fine clothes and jewelry answered the door. She grabbed the package as she yelled at the man and pushed him away. Suraj tried to hear the conversation, but he was too far away. As the man walked away, Suraj had to think fast to avoid being seen. He climbed the open staircase that led to a balcony off the upstairs rooms. He entered a well-lit room through an open window and found himself in the middle of a fine drawing room with a plush sofa and upholstered chairs. There were two round tables with the lamps in the corners. When he heard muffled noise from the adjoining room, he tiptoed to the doorway and saw a tall, beautiful girl, tending to a man in the bed. Suraj hid himself behind the thick curtain as he heard the footsteps on the hard floor. He held his breath as someone spoke to the girl—it was the same woman who had opened the front door to the strange-looking man. She had brought the package with her to give it to the girl.

After the woman left the bedroom, the girl walked in the drawing room with the package in her hand. As Suraj leaned forward for a better view, he stumbled and tripped over the windowsill, falling out the open window. The girl leaped up to grab him by his legs, and she pulled him inside. Suraj straightened himself out and slowly stood. "I apologize for my rudeness," he said awkwardly. The girl seemed stunned, unable to speak, but at least he didn't come across as someone who would harm a girl. It all happened so quickly that Miriam didn't have a chance to reflect upon how he got through the courtyard and up on the balcony. Suraj went on. "It is not my business, but I was curious about the package that was delivered here." He took a step closer, studying the girl. He had heard horrific stories about places like this—he was sure it was a brothel—and all of sudden, he lost interest in Peter and wondered only about the young girl in front of him. "You don't seem to belong here," Suraj said gently. "What is your name?"

"Miriam," she answered demurely. "Please sit down." She indicated a chair and then poured him a glass of water from the jug.

"I've been searching for my English friend, an army officer who went missing after an attack," Suraj explained. "His wife and parents are devastated by his disappearance." Then he asked the girl about the man in the bed and about the Western clothes brought by the woman.

Miriam was listening intently. When Suraj stopped speaking, she got up to close the door to the bedroom and then turned the lantern down to dim the light in the room. As she moved about the room, her long, wavy dark hair spilled down her back like waterfall.

Suraj noticed for the first time that the room was beautifully decorated with comfortable pillows and rugs. The chandelier and the curtains looked expensive. Suraj noticed the girl seemed poised and had cultured mannerisms.

She sat across from Suraj and poured herself a glass of water from the ceramic jug. She took several sips of water before she spoke. She seemed afraid to say anything. Suraj's ID card helped get her attention; she was not going to mess with the British authorities. She evaluated the risks of being honest with the army officer versus staying loyal to Begum Zara. Finally, she whispered, "You must be discreet about what I am about to tell you. I could get myself in a lot of trouble for intervening, but … the English officer you mentioned might be the man in the next room."

Begum Zara was traveling back from the city in her horse cart when she spotted someone dragging himself out from the undergrowth on the side of the road. She ordered the cart man to stop and check it out. The cart man immediately pulled the reins on his horse to bring the cart to a stop. He jumped off the cart and ran to the man, who was writhing in pain asking for help. The cart man yelled back to Begum Zara that a man in the bushes was an English man wearing a uniform and that he was badly injured.

Begum Zara got off the cart and hurried to help the cart man. With her strength, she and the cart man supported the soldier over their shoulders and brought him to the cart. They shifted the soldier, who was twice as big as both of them, onto the back bench of the cart. Then the cart man secured the soldier tightly by using the long fabric of his head turban, so that he would not fall off the seat. He then covered the soldier with a blanket and headed home.

Begum Zara had many ideas floating in her mind for how best to use this man to her advantage—it was a matter of taking care of her business. They still had a long way to go, and it had gotten dark.

Begum Zara had arranged for the soldier to be taken to the house where Miriam lived. Once there, she checked on his injuries under the lamp. He was badly injured on his head. His forehead looked swollen, and his shoulders were badly injured. The man was going in and out of consciousness. Begum Zara immediately sent for her doctor. Dr. Husain arrived quickly and did his best to stop the bleeding. He cleaned and sutured many wounds, but he was more worried about his head injury. He needed to perform more tests before he could conclude his diagnosis. The soldier was unable to speak or respond. Dr. Husain prescribed medication, and Begum Zara sent her cart man to fetch the medicines.

As Peter drifted in and out of consciousness, the attack became part of his dreams. A group of highly trained men on horses had attacked Peter and his unit in a guerilla-like warfare and confiscated their weapons and artillery wagon. Their faces were covered with their turbans except for their eyes, and they were heavily armed. Peter and his subordinate were the only two white officers. All the soldiers were on foot except for Peter, who was on horseback, and the other officer, who was in the jeep with the artillery. The leader of the attackers hustled toward Peter, pointed a gun at him, and said, "We have no intention of hurting anyone. We are here to take the artillery without any bloodshed. If you remain still and let us get on with it, my men will spare you."

Peter instructed his men to put down their weapons and ordered his subordinate to release the vehicle. He didn't want to put his men's life at risk. Peter allowed the leader and his men to take their artillery and leave. A split second later, Peter's subordinate fired shots, and the other men followed in confusion. The fleeing gang men on horses reacted by lobbing grenades at Peter and his men. Peter's horse was frightened and ran wildly around the smoke-filled area. Peter pulled on his reins, trying to control his horse, but the animal broke into a gallop. Peter's eyes were burning from the smoke and dust. A moment later, at the edge of a cliff, his horse reared violently on his hind legs, throwing Peter to the ground. Peter, his foot stuck in the stirrups, was dragged across the rocky marshland and suffered serious head and body injuries.

Begum Zara stayed up all night to check on Peter's condition. She didn't want anyone to discover the fact that an English army officer was in her custody. The cart man proved to be the only person she trusted with her secrets, apart from the doctor himself.

Begum Zara and the doctor had known each other for many years and shared other secrets. They had met years ago at a brothel run by two sisters. Zara was a young, beautiful, and talented dancer who danced in the evenings at the brothel. A young doctor, Husain, loved a Hindu girl but couldn't marry her for two reasons. For one, his religion didn't allow him to marry a non-Muslim, but more importantly, the girl's brothers would rather kill their sister than let her marry a Muslim boy. The girl was forced to marry someone else, and young Dr. Husain took to alcohol to drown his sorrows and ended up as a regular at the brothel. Begum Zara had helped the doctor mend his heart. They had grown old together, and their secrets were safe with each other.

Miriam was born to Begum Zara at the brothel, but the two sisters who ran the place forced her to give up Miriam for adoption. It was years later when Begum Zara heard that her young daughter was being forced to marry a seventy-year-old wealthy man. Begum Zara had used all the power to free her daughter. Her clients included Police Inspector Tambe; Mr. Yadav, an attorney; and some young political leaders. They all used their influence to bring Miriam back to her. Begum Zara had not mentioned to anyone in the world that Miriam was her daughter. The only two people who knew about their relationship were the two sisters, who now were dead. Even the doctor was surprised to see the pains she was taking to bring this girl home. Begum Zara, who was a very shrewd businesswoman, had done enough favors to people in business and otherwise that she was confident that in time of need, the same people would not turn their backs on her.

Begum Zara placed Miriam at her home away from the brothel, as she feared for her young daughter's future. There were plenty of vultures in society who would kill for young and fresh flesh. In times of unrest, diverse crimes took place, mainly related to drugs and alcohol. Begum Zara had noticed in her profession that crime lords were gaining power. She had to have law and order to protect her business.

Inspector Tambe and other police officers were regular clients at the brothel, now owned by Begum Zara. She continued to establish good relations with her clients, and they helped to keep her safe. Western influence on local people had damaged the Indian culture and heritage, and moral values had changed. Young people like Inspector Tambe and the others now wanted a new style of young girls—those from the city who would dance and entertain different from previous girls. Begum Zara had to change the entire outlook of her business. It was no longer a brothel; it became more like a club. Its name changed to the Piccadilly, a clean, vibrant, and modern club that drew rich, sophisticated clients. The new look of the place was to attract young people, with the help of young, modern, city girls who spoke English and knew how to entertain white men. Business doubled as cabaret dancers from Delhi were hired to perform in their glitzy dresses and high heels. Drinks were served in tall glasses with ice cubes, and modern music played instead of the traditional Indian classical music.

Begum Zara even changed her name to Zara Madam. The rumors were out among the top clients that Zara Madam was preparing a fine young lady to bring to the club. There were going to be high bids for her.

Miriam grew up in a household where her adopted father was a schoolteacher and her mother was a sweet lady who looked after little children at the school during lunch break. Miriam's adoptive parents were very fond of children, and they were overjoyed and grateful that God blessed them with Miriam. Both looked after Miriam with great care and love. They taught her moral values, showed her how to be kind and thoughtful, and showered her with gifts and attention but never spoiled her. Her father's desire for his daughter to be educated and follow in his footsteps as a teacher was never met. Both husband and wife were killed, among hundreds others, in a train wreck on their annual trip to the mosque.

Miriam was placed in the care of her father's younger brother and his wife, who had five children of their own. Miriam was fourteen years old—too young to fend for herself in a world full of cruel people. Her uncle took over the house and all its belongings in return for taking care of Miriam. She became prey to their cruelties, beatings, and abuse. Her chances to go to school suddenly came to a halt, because her uncle didn't want to pay for her school fee and books. Instead, he wanted her to work and help his wife at home, so Miriam's dream of going to school was squashed. Eventually, the greedy uncle sold his niece to an old man for three hundred rupees. The old man's house was where Begum Zara/Madam Zara found Miriam and, after working out a deal with the old man, she brought Miriam home.

Suraj asked Miriam if he could see Peter and talk to him, but Miriam refused to let him see Peter that night. "I will talk to Madam Zara in the morning," she promised.

"But why is my friend in bed?" Suraj wanted to know. "And what is wrong with him? Why has he been kept hidden for weeks?"

Miriam sighed, feeling obligated to give Suraj a few details. "He was found half dead by the roadside, and Madam Zara brought him to the house. Dr. Husain has been taking care of his health issues," she said, "but I'm afraid your friend has no memory of his past life. We did learn his name from his uniform, but Madam Zara decided to keep it a secret, as that's all she knew."

Zara had her own reasons for keeping Peter a secret from everyone. She believed she could use Peter to save Miriam from the hands of Inspector Tambe and others who had eyes for her. Inspector Tambe, who was beginning to be nuisance for Madam Zara, had to be maneuvered carefully. She had outwitted the inspector by placing a very high bid for Miriam from the unknown white suitor.

Dr. Husain had warned Zara about the consequences of keeping Peter away from the authorities, but she had decided against his advice and kept him in hiding. She realized it that sooner or later, Peter would have to be released to proper authorities. For now, however, she needed to use him as the "high bidder," to keep Tambe and others away from Miriam. The clothes in the package were for Peter's dramatic act as a rich traveler passing through the town. Zara was concerned about Tambe's recognizing Peter from his Missing Persons posters on every street corner. But Peter had lost a lot of weight and now had a beard, so he looked little like the officer in the picture. In civilian clothes, Peter looked so different that even Suraj, who spent so much time with him, had not been able to recognize him

Suraj introduced himself to Peter in the morning after he spoke with Madam Zara, who was made aware of the complications she could have with the authorities if she kept Peter in hiding. She had not realized the penalties and punishment for hiding Peter, but ignorance of the law was not going to save her. "If you let me take Peter now," Suraj told her, "I will try to influence my superiors to be lenient toward you."

Madam Zara didn't want to get involved with police and came clean with Suraj about her fear for her daughter. "Miriam has been taking care of your friend and has grown fond of him. She does not know that I am her mother." Suraj respected Zara's sentiments as a mother and felt pity for her. A sense of shame and guilt didn't allow the poor woman to accept her own daughter.

Miriam sat next to Peter, holding his hand, while Suraj tried to have a conversation with him. Suraj showed him pictures of his wife, Annie, his parents, and other pictures of him with his unit. Bewildered, Peter could not remember anything of his past. Every day was a struggle as he tried to hang on to his current memory. He couldn't deny the pictures, though—proof was right there that he was Peter McPhee, an army officer whose unit was attacked. His superiors were looking for him. His wounds were almost healed, but the scars remained.

He touched his scars on head and closed his eyes in an attempt to push himself to remember, but he blanked out. He tried to visualize his attack, so clear in his dreams, but he could not bring back the memory of that fateful incident.

Miriam had been a good nurse who healed Peter; her devotion toward her patient was praiseworthy. Timely medications, proper food, and spending time together brought them closer to one another. Her constant care and bright spirit won Peter's trust. He had become so dependent on Miriam for everything. He enjoyed her company and her candidness, and they laughed as they learned to speak each other's language.

Peter's past life had raised a few questions for Miriam, but she ignored them. She felt it was only important that he retain all his current memories after the attack. His brain seemed to function just fine otherwise. His interactions with the doctor confirmed that he was on his way to a healthy and normal life. The probability of regaining his past memory was low but not entirely ruled out.

Peter was grateful, appreciative, and indebted to Miriam, Zara, and Dr. Husain, who had saved his life and taken such good care of him. To see Peter and Miriam happy together, Zara allowed herself to dream about their union in marriage. Zara even had hope that Miriam might accept her as her mother, but she decided to wait for the right moment to announce Miriam as her daughter. Too many years had been lost, and she had to consider Miriam's state of mind. Zara had to prepare herself for a possible emotional outburst from Miriam in response to the new information. Zara feared that it might take a while for Miriam to absorb that Zara who ran the brothel was her own mother. She also feared the questions regarding her father.

Zara gathered all her courage to talk to Dr. Husain. She had been edgy and nervous all day. She sent the message for the doctor to see her in the evening. She looked stunning in her long-sleeved black-and-gold embroidered caftan, and her gold chandelier earrings looked very pretty on her. She had strikingly beautiful eyes rimmed with black kohl and long lashes, and her hair was tied up in a bun. Her passion for dance kept her physically fit for her age. She was pacing up and down when Dr. Husain showed up. He followed Zara onto the balcony overlooking her backyard.

A pitcher of cold water and two glasses of whiskey were on the table. Zara knew the doctor liked to have his whiskey in the evening. He poured the drinks and handed one to Zara. She waited for the doctor to take couple of sips and then asked him to sit down. Zara sat across him and looked straight in his eyes.

"I have some important news," Zara began, "and it concerns you too." She then disclosed that Miriam was her daughter. "Just as important," she went on hesitantly, "is that you are her father." She reminded him of the year when he first came to her, hoping to get over his lost love. His parents had been furious that he was seeing a girl at the brothel, and he had stopped seeing her for a few months. "In that time we were apart, I learned I was pregnant with your child. The cruel women who ran this brothel forced me to give up my baby girl. And that baby girl was Miriam."

The doctor was numb as he absorbed the news. As he locked eyes with Zara, they each felt a strange sense of relief in their hearts. While he had noticed a striking resemblance between mother and daughter, he hadn't a clue that Miriam was his own child. He had suffered enough loneliness and shame, and he did not care about the opinion of society or its rules anymore. His parents, who criticized him for his lifestyle, were long dead, and his siblings were long gone from his life. Zara had been his real companion throughout his life, but he was not allowed to marry her. Now, the doctor wanted to put things straight. Too many years had been wasted, and he wasn't going to waste another minute.

Dr. Husain woke up the next morning with Zara's arm slumped over his chest. The immense happiness and purpose he felt was astounding. He took Zara's hand in his own and woke her, announcing that they were going to get married and accept their daughter by giving her a legitimate name. Zara gaped at him, wondering whether he was proposing from a sense of obligation, but then she saw the love in his eyes, and she was glad to accept him as a husband. The most difficult task would be releasing this information to their daughter. To their surprise, Miriam was neither exultant nor miserable. Her life with Peter was all she cared for.

Suraj was concerned that Peter had not recognized him at all. His efforts to jog Peter's memory didn't seem to work. None of the photos or stories he'd told Peter did the trick. Peter listened very patiently as Suraj went on enlightening him on his past life, but his face was expressionless, without a trace of emotion. Dr. Husain had warned Suraj not to push Peter too hard.

Although extremely disappointed by the lack of progress, Suraj knew his first duty was to inform his superiors that he'd found Peter. He wanted to have this matter handled very delicately. He was aware of the fact that Zara was mostly worried about her daughter, Miriam. It really was a silver lining in the cloud that Miriam's identity was publically revealed as Zara's daughter and that her father was none other than Dr. Husain. Her clients were initially shocked but soon accepted the facts. News of Miriam's being Dr. Husain and Zara's daughter traveled fast to the ears of Inspector Tambe and others, and from that day onward, they never showed their faces again. When the authorities were notified of Peter's circumstances, Zara was reprimanded but because she had helped to save Peter's life, she was not punished. Peter was brought back to the army barracks for a full examination of his condition. Initially, he was very reluctant and didn't cooperate with authorities. He didn't understand why he was being dragged to the army camp. Peter had lost his personal identity, but his ability to read and write and other forms of non-emotional memory were intact. It was strange for him to find himself among other white people. His mind was like that of a child who surprised himself every day by learning new things. He believed that he had been in the army and that he was married—he had seen pictures and army papers—but he could not recollect any of his past life. He allowed his caretakers to educate him on his surroundings, his relationships with people, and his daily rituals.

The army neurosurgeon confirmed that Peter was suffering from retrograde amnesia. Peter had to go through a comprehensive set of cognitive and imaging tests. He still could not recall any event prior to his head injury. All his past-life memory was wiped out. Annie and his parents were informed that his prognosis was poor due to the severity of damage to his brain. Annie was overjoyed that Peter had been found alive but was devastated that she had lost him nevertheless.

Suraj sympathized with Annie. Nervousness and fatigue showed on Annie's face, and Suraj offered to take her home from the hospital. It was a late afternoon, and the air was sticky and warm, but the ride in the rickshaw sent a rush of cool air on her sweaty face. Traffic noise and heat in the air made it impossible for them to speak.

Annie saw Peter again in the medical center the following morning, where he was kept for further observation. Hundreds of questions filled Annie's mind, demanding answers from her husband. Would he ever recognize her? Would he be happier with Miriam? Would he come back to her if he suddenly remembered everything? *What am I to do?* Annie thought piteously. *Do I stay married to him? Does he even care?* Annie didn't ask any of these questions. She knew that Peter didn't have any answers. Annie moved away from Peter with tears in her eyes. The man she thought was her husband was a stranger to her. Peter's parents were frantic about their son's mental state; they wanted Annie to bring their son back home so that they could take care of him, but Peter strongly refused to lose sight of Miriam. He didn't care to talk to anyone except Miriam.

Suraj suggested that Annie should talk to Miriam, to make her understand the situation. "Tell her that he would be better off going back to England," Suraj advised. "The neurosurgeon's said that Peter should go home where there are better health facilities; they can't predict whether Peter's amnesia is temporary or permanent. Maybe it will be easier for him at home." Annie expressed her wish to speak to Miriam in private. She wanted to know if Miriam had any idea how their lives were interwoven.

Annie and Suraj went to see Miriam, and the three of them sat under a shady tree outside her house, discussing Peter's future. It felt strange and painful for Annie to talk about her husband to another woman.

"I don't doubt at all that you are his wife," Miriam said calmly, "but I believe that Peter was given a second life, and in his second life, he has chosen me to be his partner. It's God's will."

Annie realized it was a simple truth but hard to accept. Annie had to accept fate and took it as God's will, as Miriam had put in. She realized that one could not be asked to be loved, but she couldn't help but laugh sarcastically at Miriam's version of Peter's being born again into Miriam's life or that it was destiny.

"You may laugh," Miriam said, "but I believe Peter was saved for me." She then described his likes and dislikes, his daily routine—it sounded as if she worshipped him.

Annie considered herself a good wife, but a lot had changed, and she didn't have the strength to win him back. The final decision had to be Peter's, and he was adamant that he wanted to stay with Miriam. There was no room for discussion.

Annie would return to England without her husband. With a heavy heart, she wished Peter and Miriam the best of luck. Peter's seniors had authorized Peter to have an early retirement from his current duties with full pension. His injuries and memory loss occurred at the time of the duty that earned him an award for bravery, with a huge monetary reward. Annie didn't want any part of his pension or the reward. She just needed time to figure out things for herself—like how to get out of the marriage and how to survive. Peter was alive, but Annie thought the loss of his memory sounded as devastating as death. Annie felt very sad that Peter was lost in a delusional maelstrom.

For Peter, the accusing voices in his head hushed to the point that finally, they were simply gone. Voices and people from his past were not real. He was on track to move into his own supported-living housing. The once wild-eyed, unshaven man was now being transformed. Peter was taking various medications but was still anxious and easily frightened. He seemed happy and more at ease with Miriam around at his house. This was only possible through the emotional growth they experienced together, an important first step in attaining self-sufficiency. It was evident that Miriam's support, guidance, and compassion helped Peter to gain the resources and determination he needed to accomplish his life goals. Miriam's help was so important in his recovery process that it made him want to give something back to her. Miriam had a home with someone to love, and Peter had someone he could call his own.

1936—India

SURAJ AND ANNIE

Travel documents for Annie's return to England were
arranged by Peter's superiors. Mary had insisted
that Annie return home immediately. Peter's promise
to show Annie the best of India—its heritage sites and
monuments—had not materialized. The description of
the Taj Mahal emerged like a fairy tale in front of her eyes.
She had spent hours in researching the stunning marvels
of architecture and captivating historical attractions. She
decided to go ahead with her plans to travel to these places
before she went home.

Suraj helped Annie with her travel plans. He strongly
advised her against traveling alone, but she was adamant
and was not going to change her mind. The packing
was done, train tickets and accommodation vouchers
were collected, and Annie soon found herself sitting on
railway platform with her journal in her lap, listening
to the tepid drizzle of a spring evening. When her train
arrived at the terminal, the porter placed her luggage in

the luggage compartment above her seat and helped her into her shared cabin. She gave a huge tip to her porter, who went beyond his duty to make her comfortable and safe. He even offered to get her an English newspaper, but Annie declined it and waved him good-bye.

Just as the train was about to leave, her cabin companion arrived. His face was partly hidden under his hat, but he seemed young and athletic as he pushed open the door. Annie didn't particularly care for a company, and she hoped he would stay on his side of the cabin. The man placed his luggage on the rack above and turned to face Annie with a smile.

It was none other than Suraj. Annie shrieked with joy and surprise. She had no idea when Suraj said that he was not going to let her go alone that he had meant it. He had discreetly double-booked the entire trip.

"Oh, Suraj! How wonderful! I will never forget the generosity you have shown me."

"I'm only sorry I can't do more," Suraj said warmly. "After the ordeal you've suffered, I couldn't allow you to risk your life with the bizarre idea of traveling alone in a foreign country."

They traveled to Delhi to see India Gate, Red Fort, and other heritage sites like Qutub Minar, the tallest minaret in India. Suraj translated and explained the history behind each and every site, protecting Annie like a shield from unwanted subjects. Suraj was a perfect gentleman, and his presence and ability to speak different languages gave Annie a huge sense of security. She felt safe and protected at all times.

On the third day, their explorations took them to the famous Taj Mahal. Annie felt an absurd feeling of flirting with Suraj. She was feeling a strong attraction to his rough, brazen exterior and felt a flush of embarrassment as sparks flew in her body with amusement. Her body seemed to have failed to execute her mind's orders. Suraj noticed her eyeing him differently and on a couple of occasions, he avoided her gaze, but it gave him enough signals. He initially thought it might be the effects of the alcohol they'd had over dinner. He was taken aback when Annie drew almost undetectably closer to him on the taxi ride back to their hotel. He could feel her breath on his chest as she leaned on him. His own heart was beating faster than normal. Suraj walked her to her hotel room as she clung to him for support.

When they reached her door, the dubious look on Annie's face deepened to exasperation as she tugged him inside and shut the door behind them. She pushed him against the wall, and standing on tiptoe, she tilted her face up to reach his lips. Suraj held her back from the shoulders. Annie closed her eyes and whispered, "Please kiss me," with tears running down her cheeks.

Her long lashes lowered over her beautiful blue eyes as her breath caught in her throat. Her blonde hair made waves down her neck, making her look very seductive. Annie's sensual body touching his made him very aware of his need too. He wanted to comfort her and take all her pain away.

Just as he was getting ready to give in to her kiss, she parted her lips in anticipation. Suraj kissed them gently and then passionately as she held him tightly in her grip. He swung her around, gently picked her up in his arms, and brought her to bed. He continued to stare at her as Annie removed her shawl from her bare shoulders and peeled her stockings off under her dress.

"Would you like me to stay with you?" Suraj asked nervously.

The very thought sent a delicious shiver down her body. Annie nodded and pulled him on to the bed, where he landed without grace. Very seductively, Annie slid her hands inside of his shirt and felt the hair on his chest. She unbuttoned his shirt and drew his leather belt from his trousers in a flash. His broad shoulders and strong forearms glistened in the dim light that spilled through the window.

Suraj's conscience was swept into thin air, and he forgot where he was and what he was doing. His self-control was slipping dangerously away as he slid his hand gently up her leg, pushing her dress along with it. Annie could feel ripples of hot sensation pulsing through her. He meant to pause and regain control, but somehow, he found himself in her, pulled like a leaf in a whirlpool. He felt hungry for her satisfaction, her ecstasy, her sanity. He cupped her buttocks, squeezed them, and muttered against her. He unfastened the buttons on her dress and slid it off her shoulders, exposing her bare breasts beneath, and then gently bit on her nipples, sending shockwaves all through her body. Annie coiled and her insides melted. He eased her knees apart and adjusted himself in a comfortable position as he ripped her panties off.

The next morning, Suraj went back into his room to get ready. He was in the shower, with soap on his face and water dripping from his naked body, when he stretched his hand out, searching for a towel. Instead of finding the towel, his hand encountered flesh—it was Annie, who had come in with a breakfast tray. She took one look at Suraj in the shower, and her cheeks went rosy. She quickly set down the tray.

Annie had not experienced hot, passionate sex before last night. She was sore to the point that they canceled their plans for the rest of the day and stayed in the room all afternoon, talking and eating and making love again. They both felt that they were drawing closer to each other like two ships that fail to alter their converging courses. It was a gloriously romantic sensation, but they wondered if that was right. A sense of guilt overwhelmed Annie. It was hard for Suraj to understand her. At least with him, there was a simple linear connection between what he wanted and how he felt. It wasn't until the last day of their trip that Suraj felt wretched, wondering about Peter. And Annie felt the same way about Maya in her mind.

Questions ran through their minds. *Am I a horrible friend and a horrible husband? Am I a horrible wife? Was it possible that we were drunk and disoriented? Are we simply irrational?* They found no answer to their questions, but the sight of Annie so happy in the last few days gave Suraj a sense of gratification that he was a selfless person.

1936—India

SURAJ'S SECOND MARRIAGE

*A*nnie left for England a week later. She wrote to Suraj several times, asking after Peter, but over the years, the flow of continuous letters diminished to zero as they drifted apart during the war. Suraj did write back to her, asking for her help on understanding his wife. Maya had lost yet another baby, but this one was a full-term pregnancy. Maya had started to bleed when she was eight months' pregnant from a condition called placenta previa. She had been careful throughout her pregnancy, taking proper precautions about rest, diet, and exercise. Routine checkups at the village clinic confirmed that everything was in order. Maya looked healthy and radiant, and there was no sign of a problem until that cold winter evening when she was getting in bed with her hot water bottle. Soon after, she felt warm liquid between her legs, and she immediately tossed back the covers to see if her water bottle had leaked. She let out a loud scream, waking every member of the family. Her mother-in-law, her daughters, and her servants ran into her room to find a pool of blood in her bed. Her mother-in-law covered her granddaughters' eyes and told the housemaid to take the girls back to their bed and to call for the village midwife.

The village midwife had delivered many babies. She had tried to make Maya relax with warm milk and honey, gently comforting her with gentle massages on her tummy, legs, and feet. Maya was not in any pain or discomfort; her only worry was the bleeding. The midwife was concerned that the baby was in an upside-down position. She was hoping and praying that it would right itself, but Shanti was very fearful. She woke her husband and insisted they take Maya to the city hospital. With Shanti's quick thinking and insistence, Belan drove Maya to the city hospital in the early hours of the morning.

Maya was admitted to the maternity ward, where Shanti and Belan waited for the head nurse to examine her properly. The amount of bleeding made the young nurse very nervous. She immediately called the doctor, who ordered the nurses to prepare for a cesarean section. The doctor diagnosed Maya with placenta previa, a condition in which the placenta grows and moves to the neck of the cervix, blocking the birth canal. The doctor listened for the baby's heartbeat and realized there was fetal distress, along with Maya's excessive bleeding. Maya was wheeled into the operating theater.

Shanti and Belan silently prayed with their eyes closed, waiting to hear the news. More than an hour passed before the doctor came through the swinging doors of the operating theater. He announced that the baby—a boy—didn't survive, and that Maya was not completely out of danger; she needed a blood transfusion. Shanti held on to Belan as he tried to comfort her with trembling hands. Feelings of shock and confusion left them numb. Shanti sobbed uncontrollably at the loss of a grandson, Suraj's son. She knew how badly Maya wanted a son. She felt responsible for not taking enough care of Maya. All sorts of negative emotions overwhelmed her. She could not possibly face her son with that news.

Belan offered to donate blood, and he told Shanti to brace herself and focus on Maya's critical condition. "You must snap out of it and be strong for Maya," he ordered. "Remember that Maya is still alive and will have more children."

The doctor didn't have the heart to give them more bad news—that he'd had to perform a hysterectomy on Maya to stop the bleeding.

The entire family mourned for days. It wasn't easy for Maya to accept that her precious baby son that she had in her womb was dead, and it was removed along with her womb. Maya's dreams of having a healthy boy had become a nightmare. Instead of celebrating the birth of her child, the family was grief-stricken with the news of a stillbirth. Her breasts were full of milk, yet her arms were empty. Her grief was inconsolable.

Belan wrote to Suraj, informing him of the loss of his baby. Suraj came home straightaway to support and comfort his wife. He was pained enough, learning about the baby, but learning that Maya was not able to have another child was heartbreaking news. Suraj reminded Maya of the blessings of God in the form of their daughters every time Maya thought they were cursed by God.

Maya went through the normal stages of grieving process of denial, anger, depression, and lastly acceptance. But her next stage of grieving was not acceptable to Suraj. She wanted her husband to marry again so that the new wife could give the family a son. Suraj loved Maya and could not dream of another woman in his bed—his affair with Annie was enough to torture his conscience at times, and he could not bring another woman to live at their home. He didn't understand Maya's need for a son.

Neither Suraj nor his parents ever expressed an urgent need of a male heir. He refused to agree to Maya's unreasonable request. His parents did not support the idea either, but they weren't totally against her wishes. They respected her decision, as Maya had been persuasive in making them realize her need to have her husband's son. She even promised to look for the bride herself. She knew it was not legal for a man to have more than one wife, but she knew that lots of men had more than one wife—the marriage simply wasn't registered. It was a way of life for a number of families.

Maya's decision to compromise and give up her wifely title to the new woman was her choice. She reasoned with Suraj and his parents. She had known the atrocities inflicted upon her husband's family from the uncle and cousins in an effort to eliminate the boys, so they could have their share of the wealth. The family would be unable to transfer their wealth and land to their daughters.

Maya wasn't prepared to let anyone take their hard-earned land and wealth just because she didn't produce a son as an heir. She naturally felt bitter that her daughters, who deserved their inheritance, would have to relinquish it to their uncle Mangal's sons. She begged, pleaded, and even threatened to kill herself in order to make Suraj see her point. She didn't see herself as being stubborn but supported her decision on a matter of principle.

Suraj was waiting to hear from Annie to help him in this predicament. He somehow thought Annie would have an answer. Annie wrote back to Suraj that if he truly loved his wife, he should do what his wife needed him to do—he should oblige her. Reluctantly, a year and a half later, Maya married her husband to a girl from her own village, someone Maya had known as a young girl. The girl's parents had been dirt poor, and Maya promised to take care of their daughter. With a little persuasion and a large sum of money, the girl's parents had agreed to marry their daughter off to Maya's husband.

Suraj initially refused to have a physical relation with his new bride—he loved only Maya. He truly respected and appreciated the passion she had in order to save his family's name, honor, and fortune. He realized the sacrifice she was making by sharing her husband with another woman for the sake of a son. Maya, however, made sure that Suraj consummated the marriage with his new wife, Sheila. Suraj reluctantly agreed. He gulped down couple of shots of whiskey for nerve so he could perform without a guilty conscience.

In 1937, Suraj was sent away for vigorous training

to Singapore, as the need for troops against revolts was becoming very urgent. Fortunately, by the time he was reassigned, Sheila was pregnant, and the whole family hoped for a boy.

Maya took good care of Sheila, and when she delivered a baby boy, Suraj was informed. The entire village celebrated the birth of their son, but Maya was very concerned about the baby's health—he seemed very weak and his skin had a yellow tinge. Doctors diagnosed jaundice, for which he was treated. Still, he didn't gain weight as he should have done. Sheila was not able to nurse the baby, as she suffered from postpartum depression. Maya took on the mother's role and, without any complaint, nursed the baby to good health. Shelia suddenly became redundant, as Maya took charge of everything.

It wasn't until weeks later that the family discovered that Sheila had an addiction to opium—that explained baby's poor health. Maya was furious at Sheila for risking her baby's health. Sheila could not take any more pressure or responsibility and poured her heart out by admitting that she had not wanted to get married or have a baby. She confessed that her parents had forced her into the marriage. She told Maya that she loved someone else, but her parents would not let her marry a Muslim man.

Maya admitted to her dirty part—that she had paid a fairly large sum of money to Sheila's parents so their daughter would marry her husband. Maya felt guilty, but it was too late. Sheila was not happy with the arrangement—she still loved someone else, her husband was never there, and she didn't want to be a mother. She was very depressed and miserable. Her desire to go back to her lover, who was happy to have her back, was still very strong.

Maya realized that the arrangement wasn't fair to the girl who was so full of life, married to man who didn't care about her. As a woman, she related to her sentiments. She admitted her mistake and apologized sincerely. Maya wrote a letter to Suraj, advising him of the current news at home. With her in-laws' help, she reached out to Sheila's parents to set things right. Sheila didn't bond with her baby, because she was either too tired or stoned or just plain bitter about life. She let Maya be his mother. The day that Sheila said good-bye to her family to go to her beloved's house was a happy day for everyone.

1936—England

ANNIE'S RETURN HOME

Distraught and defeated, Annie returned home to England after six years in India. Her marriage to Peter was over. Peter's accident and amnesia left Annie in a terrible mental state and caused the greatest upheaval in her life. A sense of guilt and shame niggled at her heart because she'd been unfaithful to Peter with Suraj. Her conscience told her daily that she had sinned. She accused herself of being an adulterer, yet part of her refused to admit that the time she spent with Suraj was a mistake. Part of her was unwilling to correct that.

All her life she'd been taught to meet external expectations by following others' rules, but things were different now. She had to think and re-evaluate her choices and decision. She wasn't going to let the burden of excessive guilt paralyze her. The belief system that had been programmed in her childhood had to be replaced with positive affirmations. She had been a good, supportive wife and had taken care of her husband's needs.

She never complained or wallowed like other wives when she had two consecutive miscarriages. She tried to appear happy and content at all times while she was in India. Her husband had taken good care of her, at least the best he could, and they both had happy lives.

The dilemma she was in now was the financial split of the money. She was still married to Peter by English law. The questions about the entitlement of their bank savings and Peter's pension needed to be addressed. She decided to consult a lawyer in regards to the business of separation and divorce.

Annie had come into money when she turned twenty-five. She remembered the day she received a letter from the trust attorney, advising her of the inheritance from her parents. She had not taken any notice of the large amount while she was in India, as she didn't need it there. There was no denying that Annie felt at ease with the knowledge that she was financially secure.

She compared the two thought processes in her mind—one where she imagined Peter dead and the other where he was lost forever—but neither gave her any peace or closure. The thought of Peter's living with Miriam tortured her, but at the same time, how could she expect him to love her if he didn't even know her anymore? The grief was unbearable. Annie had to forgive him in order to forgive herself. The loneliness haunted her day and night. The feeling of emptiness and solitude made her disconnect from others around her. She confided in Mary about her affair with Suraj. Mary tried to console her and encouraged her to take life challenges as they presented themselves. "Remember, Annie," Mary told her, "holding onto someone prevents you from moving forward. I am the perfect example."

Annie found a weekend job at Selfridge's that kept her busy and also distracted her from thinking of Peter all the time, but the evenings were torturous for her. The constant reminder of her betrayal was as tough as his betrayal of Annie. At least Peter didn't have to forgive himself since he'd done nothing wrong, but Annie had a need to forgive herself for being selfish and needy for love.

The crushing despair of the affair—and with the proof that was so intense—was such that she couldn't even mourn it properly. All of Peter's memories at their apartment made her sick to her stomach. She was oblivious to any other reason for her nausea. It was not until Mary suggested that Annie needed to see her doctor that she learned she was pregnant. Mary gently asked Annie if she was willing to keep her baby. Annie was adamant that yes, she wanted to keep her baby—she would not entertain the idea of adoption; abortion was out of the question. Her need of a baby was so intense that she never doubted herself. The new experience of pregnancy excited her. The overwhelming sense of creating a life within Annie was pure joy, even with the crying spells and mood swings she experienced. She allowed herself to feel the myriad emotions caused by hormone imbalance, as the doctor had suggested. But there were some sleepless nights she lay awake with her inner demons tormenting her.

The baby's heartbeat in her belly, its sheer existence

and presence, forced her self-support system to kick in. The tiny life, a reminder of her "getting over Peter," had to be the reason for her to go on, in spite of all the added stress.

Mary insisted that Annie move back with her until the baby was born. She did not judge Annie but was concerned for Annie's welfare. Mixed-race children in England were not easily tolerated. Annie realized that she would have to carry the burden of shame and scorn from her own community. She argued that Indian society was forced to accept thousands of illegitimate mixed-race children that were fathered by British officers, yet when the same issue of an illicit affair at home was exposed, the civil world did not know how to deal with the racial prejudices. Mary agreed with her, but the hostility and discrimination these children endured was beyond their comprehension. The truth was that the label of mixed race or "half caste" was going to be pasted on her child.

Annie felt terrible for Mary, who would also be subject to finger pointing and would have to endure the cruelty once the baby was born. Both prepared themselves for the wicked world in which they lived. Friends and family assumed that the child Annie was carrying was Peter's, but when she explained that the father of her child was an Indian man, they were shocked and disgusted. Even after Mary explained the circumstances, with Peter suffering with amnesia, ignorant adults still treated Annie with revulsion and abuse. Mary's sister, Sally, and her husband—Peter's parents—also suffered the loss of their son, but they strongly disapproved of Annie.

There were two types of hospitals in West London—voluntary hospitals and workhouse hospitals. They were run by independent charities that were established for the benefit of the deserving poor. These deserving poor were respectable, working-class people who had fallen on hard times. Many women gave birth at home, but Mary and Annie were very apprehensive about home delivery. Mary checked out the maternity ward at Hammersmith Hospital, which used to be a workhouse infirmary.

Charlie was born in April 1937, a healthy little boy with curly dark brown hair, brown eyes, and olive skin. He was a picture-perfect baby, with all the toes and fingers. The immeasurable joy of holding her little baby next to her heart made Annie forget all worldly worries for a while.

Annie let Mary name her child Charlie Benson, as they had to register him. Annie had not felt right for Charlie to have Peter's last name. People sarcastically cooed something along the lines of "Oh, how ... beautiful" when they saw Charlie, as if they were discussing a new rose made from an exotic cross-breeding program. Annie ignored any sort of implied criticism. She and Charlie muddled through life and proved the theory that mixed race people were attractive and high achievers.

1939—India

WORLD WAR II

With the Second World War imminent, Suraj's blood boiled to learn that Indian soldiers were ready to spill their blood for the British in their war, yet they were being abused in their own home country. Contrary to the British, who feared a revolt in India, the outbreak of the war saw an unprecedented outpouring of loyalty and good will from Indian nationals toward Britain. Indian political leaders and other groups were eager to support the British in the war effort, since they believed that their strong support would secure them their independence.

In the early years of the war, British attitude was that it was unlikely that Indian troops would be required at all, but the role of the Indian soldiers proved to be the most crucial in the British victory. The British army suffered defeat in almost every field in which it was deployed. Under tremendous pressure from Indian nationals, the British started the process of "Indianization," by which

Indians were promoted into higher officer ranks. Suraj was one of those Indian cadets who was sent to train at the Indian Military Academy Dehradun and was decorated as a King's Commissioned Indian Officer.

Suraj had no time to think about household issues; his duty required him show his loyalty toward the British. He was required to accompany his senior officers to another revolt in the city nearby, which he handled well by negotiating and without loss of life. He understood that most Indians nationals did not generally feel content about British rule in India. He justified this in his head by thinking that perhaps they lacked discipline or good jobs or that they were just bitter. Perhaps poor knowledge of the greater economics of the country was the reason for his ignorance. Still, he noticed that Indians lacked equal job opportunities, a subject he'd avoided in the debates with Peter and Annie. He questioned why they were not allowed to advance to high positions in government service or to become officers in the army.

He understood the need when a number of Indian lawyers and professionals formed the Indian National Congress, which debated on political and economic reforms for a better future for India and to find better ways for Indians to achieve equal status with the British. Major canals for irrigation, hundreds of thousands of miles of railway tracks, and faster steamships all were engineered for the advancement of the British. Major production and engineering posts and factories were in England, not India. India was being used for its resources, and Indians were used for cheap labor. Resentment was building in Suraj's mind.

During World War I, the Indian army consisted of over seventy thousand British troops and over 130 thousand Indian troops. By September 1939, with WWII at hand, the Indian army had quadrupled to eight hundred thousand officers and soldiers. Suraj was also at captain's rank with the 9th Jat Regiment. He was among the fine Indian officers who were drawn from various races and religions, although there was a preference for the martial races from the Punjab. Indian troops served abroad in WWII, cooperating with the British government as a form of bribe to Britain to earn independence.

Suraj started taking keen interest in the news of the Indian National Congress. He was the victim of the same crime of unfairness and discrimination. He felt equal to his counterparts when it came to his physical and mental power, yet British officers were given preference. Acquiring knowledge through newspapers and media in his spare time, he became acquainted with several hidden contacts, who educated him on the current news of what the British government was offering the general public. He was aware of Gandhi's involvement in various protests. He admired the man for his nonviolent methods of fighting back. The man had led thousands of followers on a march to the sea, where they made salt from seawater, in order to disobey the British government. He encouraged the locals to make their own salt, so that they didn't have to buy it from the government, who was making huge revenue by forcing locals to buy salt off them, just as it was in the textile industry.

Suraj learned that India was being used as an assault and training base and provided vast quantities of food and other materials to British forces and to the British at home. Following the attack on Pearl Harbor and the bombing of Singapore, the United States declared war on Japan. Suraj was sent to Miami Beach near Penang, Malaysia, to fight the Japanese. Japanese planes dropped bombs and machine-gunned the civilian population. The attacks continued for three days. Suraj's unit was ordered to evacuate Penang and to guard a railway bridge. When Japanese bombers appeared, they were met by brave Capt. Suraj and a few British fighter pilots. The Japanese were forced to withdraw. But later what happened in Penang made for sad and sorry reading in the British newspapers. While in Penang, Suraj contracted malaria; he was hospitalized and sent to Singapore.

By early 1942, the Japanese had landed in Singapore, and it was apparent that the surrender of Singapore was imminent. Almost three hundred soldiers were killed and many more were wounded. Suraj, together with the second in command of the unit, had a difficult job disposing of the corpses—they dropped them in the ocean. British forces had no other choice than to surrender unconditionally to the Japanese.

The defeated and demoralized Suraj and his unit soldiers collected themselves at the POW camp. A Japanese officer in charge had addressed the POWs and expressed his firm belief that the British were using brave

Indian soldiers to fight their war. He challenged Suraj, as their leader, that their liberation as an independent India could not be achieved and maintained without a war against the British. He further said if Indian POWs were prepared to fight British imperialism for the noble cause of achieving the independence of their motherland, the Imperial Japanese government would provide its support. He suggested the formation of an Indian National Army and handed over all the POWs to the Indian National Army's leader.

Suraj had fallen seriously ill. His trust of the British army had been shattered. Once released from the command of the garrison, POWs were sent to a shelter camp, and Suraj was admitted to a POW hospital.

Toward the end of the war, the powerless, unarmed people of India came together to defy the British Empire, which had tightened its noose around a country split by religion, class, and caste. But when the united nation rallied under Gandhi's nonviolent protests, the movement of "Quit India" got such a strong momentum that it stunned the world. That was the first ever revolution of its kind in history where there was no physical fight or attack, but it did more damage to the British than they had anticipated. America too had gained independence from the British Empire and paid heavily in financial cost and lives, but their protests were physical confrontation. The truly extraordinary strength of Indian nationals was in being persistent, peaceful, and non-cooperative. There were a few armed uprisings but not many. Ordinary men and women stood up against the British Empire, valiantly facing police batons and guns. Suraj witnessed as common people marched, singing freedom songs and facing the hardships of prison. They lit up the bonfires of foreign cloth in favor of the non-cooperation movement. The suffering caused by the British as well as the failure of the British government to give India back to her people bred hostilities and fueled the campaign for "Free India."

1939—England

WORLD WAR II

With the Second World War looming, the British government began preparing for air-raid precautions with air-raid sirens. The male population of England shrank dramatically, as millions of men signed up for duty overseas, leaving young boys and old men at home. All single women between the ages of eighteen and thirty were also called upon to register. Annie, in total panic, agreed to marry Joe Hunter so that she could stay at home with Charlie. Joe was a mechanical engineer who specialized in designing naval ships. He worked at the London docks. He had met Annie at the maternity ward when Charlie was born at Hammersmith Hospital.

Annie had envied Lorraine, who was in the ward with her. She received regular visits from her mother as well as from Joe, whom Annie assumed was the father of the baby. Annie had no one to visit her except Mary. Annie begged the nurses to leave the curtains around her during breast-feeding—she wanted to hide her baby from prying eyes. She was envious of Lorraine, who had a normal, supportive family around her.

Her own self-pity repulsed Annie, and she felt guilty and ungrateful that she didn't appreciate having Mary at her side. A very sweet and kind Lorraine had seen Annie's tears and saw the way the nurses treated her with dirty looks. Lorraine was compelled to reach out to her.

When Lorraine walked over to Annie's bed on the third day and saw a brown baby, she suddenly understood everything. She held Annie's hand and told her that her baby son was beautiful. For some reason, Annie believed Lorraine. She felt her compliments were genuine and soon, they became the best of friends. Lorraine seemed to be a very positive and happy person who always cheered Annie up. She introduced her brother Joe to Annie on his next visit.

Annie felt ashamed of herself for being jealous. Lorraine's husband had died three months earlier in a mining accident. Her brother Joe and her mother were being extra supportive since Lorraine's loss had been so great. The birth of her baby was the only light in the tunnel for her.

Annie expressed her condolences and sympathized with Lorraine's situation. Coping with a husband's tragic death was a close enough experience to Annie's that she could relate. Both women felt lucky to have someone to care for them. They kept in touch and met once in a while with their babies. Joe tried to meet Annie a few times, but Annie got busy with the new baby and didn't have time to socialize with anyone.

Finally, on Lorraine's insistence, she did go out with him. She found Joe attractive, but she was unable to feel love toward him. Joe was a quiet and serious chap who was reliable, good-hearted, and practical. Realizing the necessity of a husband, she married Joe in 1940, when Charlie was just three years old.

War was raging in Europe, and families who could afford it constructed an Anderson shelter, a prefabricated air-raid shelter made of a corrugated metal frame. Joe erected one in a three-foot-deep hole in the garden. When Joe was called in to enlist for the war, Annie and countless other women were forced to survive without spousal support. It was difficult, but they persevered, often pulling more than double-duty as mother, father, and wartime factory worker. If war production opportunities were unavailable, many women made ends meet by taking in boarders, moving in with other war wives, or returning home to live with their parents until their husbands could return home. Annie was back with Mary. All women aged between eighteen and sixty were required to choose a job, ranging from factory worker to clerk or farm girl. In order to grow more food, more help was needed on the farms, and so the government started the Women's Land Army. "Lumberjacks" were sent to fight the war, and "lumberjills" took over the farms.

Mary continued to teach at the school and when the schools were closed, she worked at the factory with Annie in alternate shifts, so that one of them would always be home with Charlie. Provisions were made in factories for children, so some days, Charlie went to work with his mother and grandma, and he slept in hammocks.

Britain itself was the target of frequent attacks by the enemy. Buckingham Palace was bombed during the raid. Because much of the bombing had been done in London's East End, after the attack on the palace, the Queen famously uttered, "I'm glad we have been bombed. Now I can look the East End in the face."

Joe remembered that beautiful, sunny Sunday morning when war was declared. He was digging in the back garden, ready to put up the Anderson shelter. Annie had Charlie in her arms when she called Joe in to listen to Mr. Chamberlain's speech on the radio. It wasn't long after that the warning siren sounded. They felt so vulnerable—they imagined planes coming over and bombs dropping. Later, of course, when the war really started, they didn't have to be told that there was a raid going on.

Annie recalled one night when she hurried home and was sheltering in a doorway when a piece of shrapnel went right through her coat. The dreadful raids continued, and even after a terrible night, Annie and Joe still had to get up for work the next day and face countless difficulties. Train stations had been bombed, and buses didn't run, as there would be unexploded bombs in the road. A lot of people got rides from whoever would take them—truck drivers were very kind. The East End of London was bombed mercilessly.

Annie applied for another job, as a clerk at a place called Freemans, which was a mail-order firm. Women filled some of the openings left by men who went into the military. Joe was sent to Chatham Dockyard to help set up a fleet of trucks fitted out as repair workshops. They were then sent out to repair the motor torpedo boats that were damaged. Annie knew nothing of this; he could only tell her that he did not know how long he would be gone. Even when the invasion began, she was unaware of the part Joe was playing. Those little MTBs were marvelous; they were so fast that nothing could touch them at sea. Joe had preferred them to the Spitfires, as they were speedy and maneuverable, and they certainly earned their place in history in many of the events that helped shorten the war.

Joe was the unsung hero of WWII who was part of the Coastal Forces protection that helped win the war, but he lost his life during the process. The shocking news of Joe's death left both Annie and Lorraine in agonizing pain. Annie had no tears, dreams, or desires left in her eyes. She was done putting up with God-knows-what horrible conditions and deprivation, yet she couldn't help scolding herself. *How dare I complain?* She thought. *Everybody else is in the same boat; everyone has suffered pain one way or another.* Meanwhile, life went on. Annie continued to go to work, coped with all sorts of shortages, and learned to live with the horror that surrounded her. She listened to the news and feared for the safety of her boy. The fighting spirit that had kept England battling during the war was all gone. A couple of years later, food, coal, and petrol were rationed. Annie could not buy real eggs for Charlie. Eggs came as egg powder to which water was added—and it tasted horrid. Butter, jam, bacon, and tea were scarce. Public buildings and streets were littered and pitted with shrapnel scars. More disturbingly, the British government felt that economic blow as a flood of cash and commodities from India to fuel the war had dried up.

Annie and many others like her resented the fact that their husbands were either dead or lost, or they returned home as strangers after the war. There was a discernible trend of lawlessness—breaking into houses and vandalism. Annie was beginning to find life very hard, and the lack of a father figure at home for Charlie made her feel very insecure. Playing the roles of both parents and a provider to her son was taking its toll. With Mary's help, however, she kept the stability of home life. They played cards and board games and talked to Charlie at the dinner table.

A lot of men showed interest in Annie, but she didn't entertain the thought. Concentrating on her son became her primary goal. Neighbors' nosiness, prudishness, and policing of each other's lives were another reason Annie was put off. She could not believe how dull and how respectful she had become; she felt almost dead from the neck down.

1942—Indian National Army

$\mathcal{S}$uraj's health improved at the camp. Along with thirty important senior officers from among the Indian POWs, he attended a conference called by the head of the Indian National Army (INA). The non-cooperation movement by Gandhi Ji was interrupted and met very tough resistance by the British. Brave revolutionaries like Bhagat Singh and Udham Singh were crushed by the British. Suraj and many other young officers, who now belonged to the INA, supported the Gandhian ideals. Thousands of people, from farmers to tradesmen, took part in the rally for freedom. Suraj was impressed by Gandhi Ji's ability to convince and persuade his followers to sacrifice the comforts of life for a short period in order to gain lifetime independence. Gandhi Ji had become a role model by giving up life's comforts in order to support the principle of fundamental rights for humans and nations. His approach was very different from any ruler, emperor, or government in history.

Subhash Bose and Mohan Singh, founders of the INA, were of the idea that Indians had to be tough and fight back. They needed to recruit young, brave soldiers with passion to stand up against the enemy and fight back for their country, but the majority of India was struggling to feed its population and had little strength to fight back. Frustration and anger caused riots everywhere, and violence was on the increase. The INA leaders were provoked by the British troops. They used every power and resource to break the will of the few who were courageous enough to stand up to their injustices. British crushed them like ants, and the punishments became more severe each time as a lesson to the INA.

The time had arrived for all Indian leaders and army officers to come together. Gandhi Ji, Jawaharlal Nehru, and Subhash Bose—the main freedom fighters—revolted against Imperial Britain. Initially, Suraj officiated as lieutenant colonel of the Azad Hind, or Free India, movement. Later, Suraj accompanied Nehru to Rangoon in Burma on his mission to reevaluate the strategies of INA.

From early 1945, the strategic situation changed swiftly as war in Europe was being won. British planes bombed the INA defense camps, killing many and forcing the survivors to withdraw. The INA zones suffered daily bombing, and the British forces advanced in heavy tanks and armored vehicles. Gandhi Ji sent Nehru to talk with Subhash Bose, so he could hold his protests and propagandas against the British. His belief in truth, nonviolence, and love for his fellow human beings was picking momentum. Gandhi Ji had felt that the British were very close to leaving India. It was just matter of days, but others felt that the British were still dragging their feet, and they wouldn't leave unless they were kicked out.

Suraj, being an army officer, only knew force; his social and political tactics were not like-minded to the Gandhian way of thinking. Suraj was appointed second in command to one of the guerilla regiment. Apart from helping to raise the regiment, Suraj was responsible for training, discipline, morale, and welfare of the troops. By this time, Burma had declared war on Japan, and so the villagers did not cooperate with the INA. The British encircled the Indian National Army, who had to surrender. Suraj, as senior officer of the INA, along with other POWs were taken to the Field Interrogation Center. Later, he was sent to jail along with others.

Maya had insisted that Suraj keep his family informed of his whereabouts at all times. She was a pillar of strength for the entire family. She made the financial and nonfinancial decisions without Suraj's permission. His son, whom they had named Veer, grew up to be a strong, healthy boy, the apple of his grandparents' eyes. He was a loveable, pleasant, and well-mannered child who was extremely close to Maya.

Maya, who was quite strict and demanded discipline at all times, gave him her undivided attention, doting over him and making sure that he ate well, slept well, and studied well. Veer hardly knew his father, so Maya compensated for his share of love too. Suraj never failed to bring presents for Veer when he returned home. His wish to spend more time at home with his family never came true, as without fail, duty called and cut his trip short. Maya begged him to come home and give it up, like many of his colleagues had done, but Suraj was too involved to quit. He gave his family plenty of reassurances that they didn't need to worry about him but that he had to finish what he started.

Veer turned out to be a fine boy who did well at school. His brilliance in academics made Maya feel very proud of him. Some of his personal characteristics were identical to his grandfather Belan. His compassionate characteristics and mannerisms toward his elders and kindness for younger ones was noted by many people. His grandfather influenced and shaped Veer's adult life without realizing it. Maya had to have a chat with Veer about his real mother, after he had heard rumors around the village. He was barely ten years old, and Maya had cuddled him as he sobbed. Maya hoped that he would understand the situation one day, as a grown man. Veer never brought up the subject again.

1945—End of the World War II

After the attack on the INA, senior leaders, including Suraj, were put in jail and later transferred to Delhi, where they were interrogated by the British Intelligence Department. After Suraj's interrogation was concluded, the trial of the INA took place at Red Fort. The entire group of leaders was charged with waging war against the king. The news of the trial was widely publicized on All India radio and through the newspapers. The predictions were that the court would sentence the accused to death or life imprisonment.

Suraj's family heard the news on the radio. Belan was proud that his brave son had stood against the injustice, but his mother and wife wept and prayed for him to come home safely. Belan wanted to go to Delhi for his trial, but his ailing health didn't allow him to travel.

Taking the prevailing circumstances into consideration, the Imperial Crown decided to remit the sentences, and all defendants were released. The trial was of great significance. The publicity in the proceedings had enhanced the credibility and legitimacy of the freedom fighters and the struggle of the Indian National Army. Regular mutinies continued to break out in various parts of India and highlighted the amount of discontent among the Indian troops who were serving British Raj. The British had already started doubting the loyalty of the Indian soldiers, who formed the bulk of the troops in India. Even in San Francisco, California, and Vancouver, an Indian revolution was catching momentum. Sikhs who had settled in England, Canada, and the United States were being openly incited to return home to take part in a general uprising. The revolutionaries as well as the common people of India, along with the government of India, made a policy of non-cooperation against the British. The revolt was a product of the accumulated grievances of all these people toward British imperialism.

International pressure and an awakened consciousness of the general public forced the British Crown to step away from trouble coming its way. Afraid of further revolts in armed forces, the British planned to quickly hand over the power to the Indian political party. Rebellions and insurgencies may not have been significant, but they were definitely a psychological blow to the confidence of British government, which hastened Indian independence. The opposition and strong criticism of Hitler and his atrocities was watched by the entire world. German Nazis would be tried as war criminals in the world court. The British recoiled in horror at the thought. They had ruled India for nearly two hundred years, as compared to Adolph Hitler, who had ruled half of Europe for just a dozen years. Hitler clearly was a vicious murderer who was responsible for murdering millions of Jews, but it did not take much imagination to realize the damage the British did to India.

1947—India

INDIA'S INDEPENDENCE AND PARTITION

*I*n June 1947, when Lord Mountbatten announced his plans for partition of India, the news was taken as one of the most tragic of all political events to affect India. The British tore the country in two parts on their way out—the nation was divided along religious lines: Pakistan as an Islamic state and India as a secular one. Britain prepared for the transfer of power from the British Crown to India and Pakistan. The British left India, and there was freedom at midnight.

Suraj called home and celebrated. The birth pangs of a free nation were followed by separation anxiety. Suraj's troubles weren't over yet. He had to take care of his family's needs. His family home and land were in the part of India that wasn't theirs any more. His main interest in going home was to evaluate the damage and prepare his family for the worst. With an uncertain future, high emotions were the frightening concoction for any unrest.

He took the train home that same night and discussed

the options and thoughts of partition with his father. Belan had known all along that it was imminent and that they would have to evacuate Lahore and move to Indian soil. Even though both governments made possible the provisions for the transfer of land and wealth between the countries, the reality was far from perfect. The shock of leaving his home and land literally took Belan's breath away. Belan passed away a few days after hearing the news. Shanti could not bear the loss and took to bed.

The first train from Pakistan, which ran from Lahore to Delhi, was in August 1947 in a climate of warmth and bonhomie. However, as massive population exchanges took place between the two young nations, tensions ran high and fanned public passions. As people were plucked from their homes and forced to cart their families and belongings to the strange new land across the newly drawn border, they came under attack from bandits and hired thugs. Both inexperienced governments were ill equipped to deal with such massive migrations. Displacement and violence, with over ten million refugees, was a gigantic task. An estimated million or more died during the Partition. The scars of Partition lived on in public memory.

Suraj had to brush aside his grief at losing his father. He helped Maya pack the necessary household items in large boxes, all the while worried sick about his young daughters on the treacherous journey through troubled areas. In general, people seemed infected with a spirit of a vendetta. More than the disruption, there was genocide as members of one religion were slaughtering the other.

In particular, the humiliation of women was foremost, including raping and disfiguring women in front of their families. Suraj shared his fears with Maya. He had a lot of contacts who offered support and security for his family, but the trust in humanity was gone in that mayhem. Maya had a long talk with her daughters the night before they left. They hugged each other as they got themselves prepared for the morning, and Maya tied rat poison in the corner of their dupputtas (a light veil). She cautioned the girls that if they were caught and faced rape, mutilation, or torture, they were to swallow the poison at once. Death was preferable to capture or torture at the hands of an enemy. She showed both daughters the poison in her own dupputta and made a pact they would all go together if it came to that. Stories were rampant of Muslim men converting Hindu girls and marrying them in order to spare their lives. The refugee movement turned into a surge as millions sought safety across the border, where the community was in the majority. Hindus and Sikhs belonged to India, and Muslims to Pakistan. Home wasn't where they were born and lived all their lives but where they belonged now.

Suraj safely moved his family to his mother's brother's place in Amritsar across the border. Temporary accommodation for six people caused a lot of inconvenience for both families. Suraj's family didn't demand to be treated as guests; the family only needed a little privacy. Suraj was more than generous with financial help to his poor uncle, as he needed his uncle's help to register his allotted land in the town of Amritsar with its physical address. His resourcefulness got him a good deal. Suraj was entitled to ninety acres of land in Punjab in compensation for his father's land in Lahore, now Pakistan. Since it was nonagricultural land, he planned to sell it as commercial land at a much higher price. He had already made a decision that since he was not a farmer; he was going to move to a city or a hill station. He discussed the matter with Maya in detail.

With his mother sick in bed, he didn't like to stay at his uncle's home for longer than needed. As soon as the deal was done, Suraj made plans for the family to move to a small town on a hill station. Shanti's health deteriorated even further. With the doctor's advice, the family decided to stay where they were for few more days, hoping that Shanti would feel better. Her fervent wish to visit the Golden Temple was fulfilled the day her doctor gave her permission to travel. Suraj made arrangements for the entire family to accompany her. Overnight bags were packed for the next day. Suraj arranged two motor cars for the comfort of his family. It was an hour's ride from the village. They arrived just on time for morning prayers. Shanti was so grateful to Suraj and Maya that they had made it possible for her to visit the most sacred and the holiest temple for Sikhs. She wished she could have had her husband's company at that moment, and her only complaint to God was that it didn't happen in Belan's lifetime. She bowed down on to the ground in front of the beautifully decorated holy book, in submission to God to thank the Lord for a good life, and she prayed for her family's good health, longevity, and prosperity. She never lifted her head again.

Suraj and Maya made funeral arrangements with the help of his uncle and other relatives. The unfamiliar place gave no solace to the traumatized family. The disturbing fact that their mother was robbed of her home and had no place she could call home troubled Suraj; it felt wrong. He bought a piece of land the very next day and built a shrine in honor of his mother so she could call it her home. The transition had taken longer than her willingness to live. Within a month of her husband's passing, she joined him in the other world.

After independence, the INA had honored Suraj with medals of the highest regard. He was given a rank of four-star general. He had taken his early retirement to recuperate from the mayhem, as he wanted to concentrate on his family first; his family needed him. A week later, Suraj, Maya, and their three children boarded the train to Shimla. Arrangements were made prior to their arrival. The cultural richness and the climatic condition earned Shimla the title of the "Summer Capital of India" during the British rule. Shimla, the queen of hills, was the perfect spot, but Suraj also felt the terrible uneasiness of digesting the fact that the British had built up the city so well for their needs. The construction of railways in Shimla was the best thing for the locals. The bridge joining the two satellite villages up in the hills helped the city to prosper in business and saved a lot of travel time—schools and shops became reachable. The entire layout of the city was carefully determined by topographical conditions. The main area, which was extensively used, was the pedestrian mall atop the highest contour. It had been the main spot of rendezvous for the Englishmen, and it was where the main offices, shops, churches, theaters, and clubs were built.

Parts of southern Shimla were used as a residential area, called Chhota Shimla, meaning "smaller in size." The local businesses, grain markets, and bazaars were built just below the exclusive mall road. The ridge was mainly dominated by the church, a Gothic structure with stained-glass reinforced windows. The whole structure of the church was made of stone and was plastered from the outside. Its tall spires were visible over the skyline of the city. Another colonial structure, with its pitched roof adjoining the church, was the municipal library, which excited Suraj. The mall, which was located at the heart of Shimla, was a place where people spent time, free from the fear of being run over by vehicles. The burrows of rickety structures in the lower markets, woven together with flights of steps and narrow lanes, had a personality of their own. The entire little town had a character of its own. Locals were happy to share the gift of beautiful nature with the British who had lived there for hundreds of years, in spite of the racial prejudice. Generally, local people spoke well of the British, praising them for doing well for their city.

Suraj was glad that he made a good choice in selecting Shimla as their new home; he had traveled a lot during his service to the country and had not seen a prettier sight than this. He appreciated the architectural gift from the

British and was hoping that perhaps one day, his own countrymen would take up the good work the British had left behind. The mayhem and destruction he witnessed made him question, however, if his people would ever get over the hatred and heartache from the partition. The violence and disorder he witnessed left a little doubt in his mind that two new nations needed a ruler for tough discipline and direction.

The earlier lifestyle of British officers and their wives who visited during long summer breaks was one of indulging in pure comfort and luxury in the company of their fellow men and women. Together, they formed the Shimla Society, the membership to which was an exclusive privilege earned by couples who were considered the cream of the crop. The city was very expensive, and had limited accommodations. The presence of many bachelors and women, who passed the hot days there in cool comfort, gave Shimla a reputation for adultery and gossip about frivolity and intrigue.

Suraj needed to explore Shimla to find a fine suitable home for his family. He decided to rent a small home on the outskirts of Shimla. It was a compact house with plenty of storage space, a large kitchen, and a fireplace in the sitting room. The fireplace was the best feature for Maya, as it was needed for the cold evenings. Maya had not traveled much or had experience with the new way of life in a city. Suraj wanted a good life for his family with his new fortune. He purchased a motor car and drove his wife and kids to places they had never been. Maya and her children tasted soft drinks and other fancy foods for the first time. The idea of eating out and staying overnight at an inn seemed like such a waste of money for Maya, but Suraj insisted on being frivolous, and Maya obeyed. She soon developed the taste for it and never complained again.

Maya and Suraj's daughters, Bani and Geet, were their pride and joy—fine young women who received a lot of attention from the locals. Bani and Geet were tall and lean, and their fair skin and delicate features made them appear as foreigners among the locals, who were short and stout and had slanted eyes. A number of families were in correspondence with Suraj with regard to their daughters' alliance with their sons. Suraj wanted his daughters to achieve higher education, but Maya was keen on getting them married into good families. Suraj and Maya often disagreed on issues like that. Maya had developed a strong sense of judgment in making decisions for her children in the absence of her husband. She knew what was best for them. Suraj still insisted that the girls were too young to marry and wrote to the prospective families to wait for couple of more years.

Suraj's son, Veer, was beginning to take interest in his father's life, spending time with him in the evenings after school, listening intently to his war experiences (although Suraj left out the gruesome parts) and general stories of his travels. Suraj fixed things around the house, and Veer was always there as an assistant. Suraj insisted on routine, self-discipline, and order. He organized his office and helped Maya with the cooking and other kitchen duties. Maya was set in her ways and liked the way she did things, but Suraj couldn't help showing her new and easier methods. Both tried to control each other, but they ended up laughing. Appreciation of each other and their growing love bonded them even more.

The rental house Suraj chose was like many other houses in the town that once had been the properties of British army officers. These homes became the property of the Indian government and were rented to tourists or turned into inns and hotels. Maya got busy with setting up her home with the help of her teenage daughters. Suraj found good schools in the area, for he wanted to concentrate on his son's education. He was already feeling guilty for staying away from home while his children were growing up.

Maya never complained or thought about her past. If she did miss her home at the farm, she never showed it. She was happy to have her husband home—that more than compensated for any farm or wealth she'd ever had. Life started to look better for the Singh family.

1947—Edinburgh

ANNIE, CHARLIE, AND MARY

In 1947, when Charlie was almost ten years old, Annie decided to move to the countryside in Scotland with Mary. There was no pressure from Mary, but her need to move closer to her only sister in Scotland was a better option for Mary. She was tired of work and war and wanted to retire away from the city. Annie had better job opportunities in London, but she chose to accompany Mary. She was also getting tired of the city life and the housing problems. Traffic was getting worse, and crime levels were on the rise. Annie wanted to raise Charlie in a more relaxed and safe environment, where he could use his full potential and gain a good education.

In the aftermath of the war, proper etiquette was still strong in British society. It was still "Mr. this" and "Mr. that" in most offices, and it was very hard for Annie to avoid the culture of uprightness and conformity. The dress code was crucial, no matter how uncomfortable. The formal stuffiness and lack of gaiety in clothes made Annie feel stifled. After spending time in India and observing the totally different culture, she had learned to appreciate clothing that was comfortable.

There was a world of difference between the people in Britain and people in India. In India, Annie had noticed people generally expressed themselves better; they were less judgmental and more hospitable and happy to be around other people. In London, she remembered crowds streaming quietly, in an orderly fashion, at the London underground. There was often pin-drop silence in the pubs, restaurants, and buses—it was utterly dreary. Such an extreme and prim way of life forced her to think about what was important in her life.

Every year, Annie bought Charlie his favorite Airfix Spitfire model plane from Woolworth's on his birthday and baked a chocolate sponge cake. Charlie also enjoyed the comics, such as *Ace Pilot* and other adventure books. Annie and Charlie were affectionate with one another, but there was no snuggling, no curling up in a lap and falling asleep. Annie always maintained a physical distance, even though she kept her sense of humor alive. Charlie grew up to be a fine young man and made his mother proud. She put her entire inheritance in a trust fund for Charlie's future, except for the amount she spent on a comfortable bungalow and the basic necessities. Charlie finished his schooling and was sent to London University for higher studies.

1955—London

CHARLIE

Charlie enrolled in the Bachelor of Arts course at Royal Holloway's campus in 1954. The college's location was less than twenty miles from the Waterloo station, where he had got off the train from Edinburgh. It was another short train ride to Windsor, and then a cab ride to Egham was end of his journey—and the beginning of his new life. The college ran a variety of academic degree programs. Charlie chose the course that interested him the most: English literature. It was hard to rival the cultural and artistic opportunities in London, with the excellent theater and strong musical traditions. Charlie spent much of his time visiting many of London's world-renowned galleries and museums, which held items of historical importance. He enjoyed the vibrant and exciting city of London, with its historical monuments—the Tower of London, Big Ben, the Houses of Parliament, the bridges, Buckingham Palace, the cathedral, and Hyde Park were just a few of the regular spots he visited. London was a noisy, dusty, cluttered, colorful, cosmopolitan city that had a rhythm of its own. In the buzzing streets above and the noisy underground, people moved around quickly and efficiently. Students busied themselves with school courses, yet there was still time for student pranks. Charlie and his friends had to learn long quotations from Shakespeare's plays, and late in the evening, they would wander around the streets and shout the passages menacingly at passersby.

Charlie joined the student union, as it helped him with a range of issues, and an array of facilities and resources were available for students. Charlie, in more liberated society in the '50s, wore slim ties and suede shoes. He had acquired a girlfriend who wore a ponytail and eye makeup; she also was English major. She was a bright and independent girl who loved American rock-and-roll music and boogie-woogie. She was the only girl Charlie knew who wanted to play a musical instrument in a professional band. She had taken up the flute and was making steady progress, with the aid of a music book.

It was few days after she began practicing when the other members of the household solemnly presented Charlie with a petition, asking him to stop his girlfriend, Linda, from making such a hideous noise, or at least to go somewhere else to make it. Charlie and Linda took no notice but instead sang the song lyrics loudly, "How much is that doggie in the window," and had a blast.

Charlie's popularity grew among his peers, and his passion for studying English literature never faltered. In 1960, he graduated with honors. Mother Annie and

Granny Mary were present at the ceremony; Charlie had his pictures taken in cap and gown with his family. Overjoyed at his success, all three of them went to a pub for drinks. Annie met Linda and her parents, but she kept her opinions of them to herself, and they didn't show any disapproval of her either.

Social etiquette in young adults was relaxed. The young people's wild lifestyle, with American influence, was seen everywhere. "Trust and let go" was still Annie's formula, and now she wished Charlie and Linda the best. Charlie discussed his plans for research in Shakespeare and Renaissance literature and his desire to earn a PhD in literature. Cambridge and Oxford Universities were begging Charlie to join them. All sorts of prospects were within his reach.

Charlie completed his PhD in 1963 while he was at Oxford. As he moved on in his studies, he also moved on with girlfriends. Annie was pleased with his choice of a current girlfriend, Joan. She knew they were serious because Charlie never brought up the topic of any of his girlfriends before her. Joan was sweet, intelligent, and independent, and she showed a lot of respect to Annie. Annie wanted to see her son settle down with someone who cared about him—a lot of girls were self-absorbed, lacked of discipline, and indulged in music and fashion to an extreme. Joan was none of those; she was a smart, elegant lady who understood the role of a wife and a friend.

1960—London

VEER

*S*uraj and Maya were thrilled with their son's graduation from college. Veer wanted to pursue a career in medicine, which made his parents very proud. He earned a national scholarship to study medicine in London. Veer Dillon became a member of the Imperial University–London class of 1960 and was awarded the Dean's Medal. In 1962, he met a distinguished Oxford professor, known for his studies of hypertension and the physiology of blood vessels. Veer had participated in the subject at the Modern Medicine symposium at his college. The following summer, he accepted his professor's invitation to do a summer internship in his lab at Oxford. He went on to complete his MD at Oxford, followed by residency training in internal medicine at Hillingdon Hospital and then two years as a clinical associate at the National Heart Institute.

Veer became a fine physician at the age of twenty-eight. He was a devilishly handsome and most eligible bachelor and was sought after by herds of young and beautiful women. He saved himself, however, for the love of his life, Sapna, a fellow physician who had been on the same path of as Veer, as she wanted to prove that she could achieve her goals as a woman. Her family was supportive of her traveling alone to England in search of better prospects and experience abroad. Veer met her through a friend during his residency.

There was a lot of pressure from her family, especially as they now had been together for more than three years, for Veer and Sapna to commit to each other in marriage. Veer's plan was to meet Sapna's family in Delhi, India, and then proceed to Chandigarh to inform his parents of his plans to marry Sapna. Suraj and Maya had moved to Chandigarh, a modern city not too far from Shimla, seeking better living. Suraj's coughing due to damp weather was getting worse, and Maya also had enough of the fog and the chilly weather. They built a comfortable house in the foothills of Chandigarh.

Veer had begged his parents to join him in London, but Suraj still hadn't forgotten the wounds inflicted upon him by the British. Even though the relationship between the two countries was on the mend, Suraj vowed not to set foot in England. He didn't interfere in his son's decision to where he wanted to study or work, but he remained anti-British. When Veer was presented with full scholarship to go to England, Veer could not turn down the offer. Veer's entire career would have been ruined if he didn't go to London, and Suraj would not impose his personal beliefs and opinions on his son or be a hindrance to Veer's success in achieving his goals. Maya and Suraj had wished their son happiness and sent him off to England.

In 1966, at the age of twenty-nine, Veer had returned home to get married to Sapna. The wedding was a grand event in Delhi, and after spending a month at home with his parents, Veer and his new bride flew back to England and got busy with their daily work schedules; later, as babies arrived, they got busier with their family. Maya and Suraj satisfied the hunger of their empty hearts with the wedding albums and then with the smiling faces of their two grandchildren.

Veer's twin boys were growing fast, and every year when they visited India, Suraj measured them against their veranda's white wall, showing the marking of their last year's height. When the twins started school, and Veer and Sapna's work commitments increased, Veer begged his parents numerous times to visit them. They were retired and had more time. Maya missed her son and the grandkids, and so she visited them alone few times, but Suraj stubbornly refused to go to England.

1975 — India

CHARLIE'S VISIT

Suraj was diagnosed with cancer in April 1974. He had been coughing a lot, and after Maya pushed him to see the doctor, it was confirmed that he had adenocarcinoma of the lung. The news left them numb for a few days. They never expected it to be the cause of their concern. Cancer was something that happened to other people. The stigma was so strong that Maya couldn't even share it with her own children.

Suraj was generally in good health and had no other complaints. He underwent a lobectomy—a removal of a portion of defected lobe—for lung cancer. It was a major surgical procedure that required general anesthesia, hospitalization, and follow-up care for weeks. Maya didn't know how to cope with it. The despair and negative feelings because of cancer were common reactions for both her and Suraj, but Suraj also suffered after the surgery, coping with side effects of the therapy and facing an uncertain future. He felt he'd failed Maya again.

Maya quietly struggled to survive the feeling of depression and anxiety. She felt angry and fearful. With the unpredictable future and Suraj's living on borrowed time, as the prognosis wasn't looking good at all for Suraj, they decided to inform their daughters, who were distraught by the news and immediately made plans to visit him. Suraj didn't want Veer to find out about his disease, fearing he would leave his work and return home to India in a heartbeat. Suraj didn't want Sapna and the kids to suffer in Veer's absence.

Maya was badly shaken up by the visits with her daughters and grandchildren. She was trying hard to be brave for everyone, wiping away her daughters' tears, handling the housework, arranging hospital appointments, and supporting Suraj, who was so frightened of the disease that he acted like a little boy, always wanting Maya by his side. He often admitted to Maya that he was more scared to die like this than he ever was when he was fighting in the war.

Maya often told him that he was the bravest man who fought in the war, because that's what he had chosen to do. "Now your purpose is to be at home with your family," she said, "and you are rightfully scared for leaving us behind." Maya's own words had brought tears to her eyes.

Another panic in Maya's life was when, a few days later, Maya found a letter on the floor by Suraj's chair. He had fallen asleep in his chair, and the letter had fallen out of the book he was reading. The envelope with an overseas stamp drew her attention. Maya picked up the letter and saw that it was written in English. She had limited understanding of written English, but she tried to read the letter. She could tell it was from a woman named Annie, who apparently had written to tell Suraj that she had something to tell him, but she wanted to see him to tell him in person.

Suraj woke up as Maya was folding the letter back in its place. Her eyes questioned him to explain Annie. Suraj signaled her to take a seat next to him, and he told Maya everything—from his friendship with Peter and his mini-affair with Peter's wife, Annie, and all the circumstances in which the affair occurred. He had written to Annie after lot of years just to say that he had often thought about her and Peter, and wondered if Peter ever regained his memory. He also shared his health issues, fearing that he might not live long to say good-bye to her. Maya wasn't angry about his association with Annie; in fact, she suggested he invite Annie to India.

Annie had received Suraj's letter and decided to visit India to see Suraj and Maya in September 1974. The idea of meeting Maya for the first time made Annie nervous, but she was pleasantly surprised by her pleasing personality. Suraj had grown older and weaker. He had gray hair and was a little thinner, but he still looked handsome. Annie had initially gasped when she saw him, forgetting the time gap of twenty-eight years. Suraj had the same reaction on seeing Annie. She too looked thinner, but her hair still was beautiful and her eyes still were bright. They didn't pretend to be strangers. Exhaustion, struggle, and sadness had taken its toll on Annie too, but beneath the surface, she was the same girl Suraj had known over a quarter of a century ago. Her wry observation of life and people, sound judgment, self-sufficiency, and realism still impressed him.

The combination of compassion, sympathy, and delicacy were just some of her feminine virtues. Suraj ordered his kitchen staff to make Annie's favorite dishes, from what he remembered years ago, and Maya laid the table, with Annie's help. They sat on the veranda to eat, talk, and laugh. It was then that Annie told Suraj and Maya about Charlie.

Suraj was shocked, but he smiled at Annie as he held Maya's hand in his and lowered his eyes so he could hide his tears. Maya and Annie exchanged glances; nothing was said between the two, but everything was understood. The irony was that Suraj had two sons but neither from his wife, and Annie had had two husbands but neither of them was her son's father. Annie apologized to both of them for keeping Charlie a secret—she had her reasons, one of them being a fear of losing him. But she already had disclosed the information to her son and now to his father. It was time Suraj knew that he had had a son with her too.

"Would you like to see a photograph of Charlie?" she asked Suraj. Suraj nodded his head as Annie showed him Charlie's picture that she carried in purse. Suraj put on his spectacles to take a good look at his son. He looked a lot like him. Suraj informed Annie that he had married for the second time for the sake of a son, and then he laughed. Annie remembered his writing to her, asking for her opinion. Maya picked up Veer's framed picture from the side table and handed it to Annie. Suraj, Maya, and Annie sat for hours, talking about their sons. It was a relief that all three of them had lived enough life that they now were amused by the situation.

Maya felt the same comfort in Annie's company as she felt praying at the temple. Prayers had become her spiritual tool at the time of Suraj's illness. Maya wondered if Annie had appeared in her life in the form of God to engage her ability to hope. Prayers had allowed her an opportunity to articulate her hope for healing her husband, but Annie's reassurances gave her the confidence that in the worst case, she would be able to go on in life and that the pain of losing someone heals itself with time.

Annie helped to lift Maya's morale and taught her to savor the beautiful moments of closeness with her husband. Maya felt a sense of calmness around Annie. Maya had not been able to share her fears or anxieties with her own daughters, let alone with anyone else. She cherished her love for Veer and related to Annie how Annie was toward her son, Charlie. Both talked about Veer and Charlie and their successes; Maya showed Annie the newspaper cuttings of Veer receiving awards and recognition in Europe. All the cumulative situations contributed significantly to Annie's encouraging Charlie to visit his father in India.

Annie returned to Edinburgh after saying her good-byes to Suraj. Maya tried to be very positive about Suraj's treatment. He was undergoing chemotherapy but was not responding well. There were times Maya felt very lonely and isolated. Every single minute of her life was devoted to looking after Suraj. She continued with her daily chores without complaint, as she did all her life. It wasn't hard for her, because it was out of habit that she served her family's needs first. All her life she concentrated on her family and never paid attention to herself. She never tried to seek the friendships of other women. She didn't know that such a relationship existed between women until she met Annie. Maya had not realized that she was so expressive with her emotions. It proved to be very therapeutic when she had cried openly in front of a stranger, yet Annie felt like family.

Maya missed Annie after she left India. She missed their heart-to-heart conversations, talking about their struggles while their husbands were away during war, and their reasons for certain choices and actions. They both tried to comprehend the sardonic truth of their lives: that Annie had two husbands and neither of them was her son's biological father, and Maya had two sons and was not the biological mother of either of them. They smiled at each other as they accepted that God had his plans.

As it happened, Veer and Charlie were on the same flight, heading to Delhi, two brothers from different mothers who had no knowledge of each other's background, yet they sat next to each other on the plane and talked nonstop for hours about their careers. It wasn't until they exchanged their business cards and talked a little about their families that Charlie mentioned his reason for his visit. Veer respected that Charlie was on his way to see his dying father, whom he had never met. Veer didn't want to embarrass or intrude further, and left it to that, with the promise that they would be in touch when they got back to England. Charlie glanced at Veer's business card—"Veer Singh Dillon, MD"—before he placed it in his wallet. He realized that Singh was a very common name, usually used by Sikhs as a middle name. He shook hands with Veer and said good-bye to his newfound friend.

Annie had informed Charlie about his father when she returned from India. She had never revealed the truth about her affair with an Indian soldier, but now she explained it to Charlie and told him that his father's health and other circumstances had changed drastically. Maya's recent letter confirmed that Suraj didn't have long to live and wanted to see his son. Charlie was a bit reluctant; it took him several days to digest this information. He discussed his dilemma with Joan, who encouraged him to go. Charlie finally admitted to an urgent need to meet his biological father. Was it because he now was a father himself? Could he forgive his father, who didn't even know he existed? He had asked his mother for a picture of him, which Annie showed from a very long time ago. A sepia photo of two young men in army uniforms jostled his nerves. It didn't take long to figure out who the men were. Both Peter and Suraj, young and handsome in khaki shorts, knee-length socks, hats in their hands, and rifles hanging on their shoulders, were leaning their backs against the bumper of the army jeep. Annie had not taken any pictures of Suraj on her last visit with him.

She wanted Charlie to first see his father the way she remembered him, not old and shriveled.

Maya had arranged for their driver to pick up Charlie from the airport. A short, stout man with a moustache, wearing a white uniform, stood with Charlie's name on a cardboard plaque. When Charlie approached him, the man quickly led Charlie to the car, where he settled himself for the four-hour drive to Chandigarh. Charlie was keen to reach Suraj's home before dark. Annie had told him that not many drivers adhered to the traffic signals, and some drivers drove in the opposite direction on a dual carriageway, totally unaware of the dangers of a head-on collision. Charlie closed his eyes on few occasions as the driver sped along. "God save us," Charlie whispered nervously. His driver made him laugh when he said, "Sir, we have too many gods in our country to save us."

The constant blasting of horns gave Charlie a headache, but it seemed necessary for driving safely in India—to warn others that a car was approaching, as drivers did not use the rearview mirrors. Most bizarre of all was the animals occupying the streets in New Delhi—cows, elephants, camels, and water buffalo stoically making their way in traffic. And then, there were dogs and monkeys, racing along the streets.

Having inhaled traffic fumes, Charlie was feeling a little nauseated. It was dusk by the time Charlie reached his father's home. Streetlights and house lamps had come on. Chandigarh was surprisingly very neat and clean city with clean air.

Father's house was a fairly big building, built in 1960, a double-story house with exterior walls decorated with stone work. The cemented driveway at his father's house had pink borders that matched the brick wall around the house and led to the large garage with double metal doors. Another continuous pathway led to the front of the house through the front lawn, which was beautifully manicured. Even in the dim light, Charlie noticed the flower beds filled with roses, miniature hedges, and a huge heart-shaped fountain in the middle of the lawn. The wide veranda attached to the main house was elegantly designed with white marble pillars and polished marble floors. The house was of a modern architecture, with all the facilities and comforts of the European world.

Maya was waiting for Charlie at the front door. She welcomed Charlie with a smile and also said a prayer as she held a platter of sweets to welcome Charlie. Annie had informed him of Indian rituals and expected him to respect them.

Charlie's first impression of Maya was of a strong but sweet lady with a genuinely caring nature. She was taller than Charlie had imagined her to be. Suraj was waiting for him in the drawing room. The sight of his father in the wheelchair sent a chill through him. The broad shoulders and strong physique of the man in the photograph had now shrunken to small body of bones. Charlie wondered idly if his mother had loved his father; she clearly cared for him enough to come to India to see him.

Charlie bent down to extend his arm for a handshake, but Suraj extended his both arms to embrace him. He grabbed him in a quick, impulsive embrace and held him for a long time, overcome by emotions. Charlie remained in his embrace until his father released him. He saw his father wipe his tears, and Charlie too was caught up in the sentiments, along with Maya, who slipped out to leave the two men alone in the drawing room.

The next day at noon, Maya's daughters and their families arrived, but Suraj made everyone wait until Veer got home before he introduced Charlie—he wanted everyone to meet him all together. Veer's car pulled in the driveway, and the driver got his luggage out. In couple of long strides, he was standing on the veranda as Maya came out to receive him. Maya hugged her son and tried unsuccessfully to hold back a dreadful squeal—all the pain and suppressed fear came out as she looked in her son's eyes, confirming that his father didn't have long to live. Veer recognized how scared and emotionally drained she was at that point in life. Maya, who had always failed to hide her fears from her son, had no idea that Veer had already planned to take her with him to England and wouldn't leave her to be alone anymore. The emotional imbalance had taken its toll, and she collapsed in her son's arms. Veer brought her in the house and helped her onto the sofa. He hugged his weeping sisters and then approached his father and greeted him by touching his feet. It wasn't until Charlie came forward from behind his father's wheelchair and stood in front of him that he recognized the man from the plane. Perhaps it was the bright sunlight that had blinded Veer when he first entered the room full of people, because Charlie had been standing there all along, next to his father's wheelchair. Charlie, too, was astonished at the coincidence of meeting his half-brother on the plane.

Veer wondered why his new friend from the plane was at his parents' house … and then he remembered Charlie had mentioned meeting his dying father for the first time. "Oh, my Lord" were the first words from Veer's mouth. He silently looked around to see everyone's reaction and then went straight back to his mother.

Suraj had lost a lot of weight since Veer had last seen him few months ago. His sisters had informed him of their father's condition, and he had flown to India right away to see him to make sure that he was receiving the right treatment and to support his mother. He wanted to take them both to London, but Suraj wouldn't hear of that. Veer had been in touch with the oncologists on the phone on a weekly basis, going over the treatment plans; he knew the prognosis was poor.

In the last few months, the cancer had spread to his bones, which forced him to use a cane to walk and eventually a wheelchair. He had a couple of bouts of pneumonia, complications from the lungs. His health took a huge downhill slide, and he was put on oxygen. Each day he had such a drastic change in appearance and disposition. Only Maya could feel his pain. He was once her Prince Charming—handsome, strong, and beautiful—and now this man had shriveled into a tiny bag of bones. The silent suffering of her husband was unbearable for Maya. It was not only cruel to see him suffer, but she felt agonizing guilt for her own living.

Maya often enfolded him and patted his back, murmuring the reassuring phrases that one mumbles to a child who has woken up in the night, frightened by imaginary monsters in the darkness. Each morning, Maya had a routine where she washed him and dressed him in clean clothes. He wore his watch and spectacles as he sat in the wheelchair, reading his books and newspaper.

Veer looked in her mother's eyes as she introduced Charlie to her children as their father's son, their half-brother. Everyone was shocked when she told them about Annie's visit a few months back. She had kept that a secret until the time was right. Everyone hid their individual sentiments, including Charlie. Maya protected her husband from questioning eyes and told everyone that their father didn't know about Charlie until few months ago. She didn't want her children to think less of their father. Fatherhood was suddenly being snatched away from him, and it was a cruel theft. His protestations of love for his children made everyone weak in their knees. Veer remembered how his father always spoke to his mother with a note of tenderness in his voice. For forty-seven years, he had loved and admired her unwaveringly and with absolute consistency. And she had reciprocated.

Geet and Bani also saw their father's distraught and apologetic look, and they pitied him. They greeted Charlie with a smile, welcoming him to their family. Veer walked up to his father and sat in his feet. His eyes met his father's, and Veer saw a strange kind of affection for him, a language that could not be spoken but only understood, as if he was saying, "Take care of my family for me, including your long-lost brother." Veer took his father's hand, kissed it, and made a secret promise that he would do everything in his power to hold this family together. Suraj simply nodded at both of his sons and signaled to Maya to take him to his room.

Veer approached Charlie and shook hands with him, and Charlie gave him a light hug. Maya filled in the details later as they sipped their tea in the afternoon. Charlie was few months older than Veer, both born in 1937. Veer wanted to know about Annie, and the two of them talked for hours. Their half-sisters Bani and Geet were a little shy in the beginning but by the evening, they were talking freely while sitting together after their evening supper. Bani's and Geet's children became quite friendly to Charlie and soon became comfortable calling him Uncle Charlie.

Maya was at peace seeing her children getting along. She felt exhausted; all the anxiety, and worries had drained her of physical and emotional strength. She took leave to go to bed, and she checked on Suraj, who was sound asleep. His breathing was shallow as he slept with his mouth open, but he still had a handsome face with broad features. His big hands were folded on his chest, as always. Maya tucked him in, kissed him on his forehead, and slept on her side of the bed. She fell asleep as soon as her head hit the pillow, a sense of relief with her family around her helping her drift off to a deep sleep that she had been deprived of since Suraj's illness.

It was six in morning when she woke up to the noise of Suraj's manservant dragging his feet along the floor as he brought the bed tea in the morning. He was walking around the bed, huffing and puffing, when Maya opened her eyes to find Suraj dead on the bed next to her. His oxygen mask was still attached, but he was not breathing. Maya let out a scream, and within minutes, the entire household had gathered in their room. Veer and Charlie took control of the situation and got Maya and their sisters to calm down. They asked the servants to take the children back to their rooms. Veer sent one of the servants to fetch the priest and then made appropriate arrangements for the funeral.

Charlie was astonished by the funeral rituals, from taking the body draped in a white shroud to the funeral site, where it was placed on a massive heap of saffron wood logs. The priest then asked Charlie to walk around the funeral pyre with an earthen pot that had holes in it for water to sprout. Veer followed him, and he was handed a fire torch to light the funeral pyre, which instantly burst into an insatiable fire that churned out ashes for hours. The fragrant smell of saffron mixed with burning flesh made it bearable for all to breathe. It was quite an experience, an amazing way to say good-bye to one's soul.

Back at the house a ceremony of celebration of the completion of life was conducted. Everyone present at the service wore white clothes. It was a peaceful ceremony, where the priest recited the soothing mantra for the deceased. When he performed the last rites, he called upon Charlie, an elder son, to do the honors. Charlie, who was numb at that point, could not believe that he was put forward to do this task for his father. When the priest translated the verses to him in English, Charlie burst out crying. The honor that Maya, his half-brother, and his sisters had given him by accepting him as a big brother was overwhelming. Maya wanted to honor Charlie with this privilege, but she first had asked Veer and her daughters and sons-in-law how they felt. Nobody had any objection. In fact, it was very kind of them to choose this way to make Charlie feel welcome and a part of the family.

The priest placed a turban on Charlie's head to symbolize the responsibility he would take on—to keep the family pride intact. This single but powerful ritual sent an important message, making Charlie realize the importance of duty to his family. He thought of his own childhood, growing up without a father figure. Thought of his daughter Sasha, who depended on him for protection, guidance, and love, opened a lid to the emotions exploding in his head. It brought memories he had stored for years. He had not valued his mother, Annie's, sacrifices in a true sense until now. He understood that to take responsibility as a parent and of a parent is the purest and most divine task for all human beings.

About the Book

et in the historical era of British Raj in India, the story details two women's struggles and sacrifices before, during, and after World War II. Annie survives the trauma of neglect and abuse in her childhood but finds love in her husband, Peter, an army officer who is sent to India under the imperial Raj to control the constant threats of mutinies erupting all over India during the "Quit India" movements. After spending six years of their marriage in India, Annie loses Peter to a local woman, who finds Peter half dead after an attack by the freedom fighters. Peter, in a state of amnesia, doesn't recognize Annie and chooses to be with his caretaker, Miriam. Devastated and desolate, Annie finds solace in Peter's friend and fellow army officer Suraj, who helps her through the ordeal.

Suraj, a valiant and adept army officer, is sent to fight the Japanese in Malaysia during WWII and is badly wounded. From the POW camp, he is handed to Indian revolutionaries to fight against the British. Suraj, who realizes the exploitation and atrocities of the British, turns rebellious and joins the Indian National Army, formed by the freedom fighters.

Suraj's wife, Maya, who lives in a village with her two daughters and elderly in-laws, desperately wants a son. Her attempts to have a son fail tragically when complications in pregnancy lead to a hysterectomy. Fear of losing Suraj's inheritance to his mean nephews for lack of a male heir leaves Maya no option but to marry her husband off to another woman in a hope for a son.

Back in England Annie, unprepared for racial prejudices in a civil world, gives birth to Suraj's son Charlie. She carries the burden of shame and scorn, but with Mary's support, raises her son singlehandedly. During World War II, when all single women had to be registered and sent to help in war causes, she marries her second husband, Joe, who also gets killed in the war.

Annie, who has kept her son a secret from Suraj all her life, feels obligated to disclose this important information before Suraj dies. Maya is left to introduce Charlie to her daughters and son, Veer (from the second wife), and honors Charlie by allowing him to perform his father's funeral rites.

Maya's devotion to her husband and family intrigues Annie. The two remain friends forever. Ironically, two brothers from different mothers meet on the same flight but are clueless that they are visiting the same dying father.

About the Author

*B*orn in India, raised in England, and currently residing in California with my wonderful husband of thirty years, I am a mother of three adult children who have flown away, leaving the nest empty. My new adoptive family of two dogs and a cat keep me company these days. They are far less demanding, which is a blessing.

This book was totally inspired by real heroes in my family. I wanted to share my incontestable experience of cultural backgrounds of three continents and the ethnicity, richness, and incredible history with readers from all walks of life.

My debut novel is a tribute to my amazing mother who motivated me with this project. Listening to her stories made me want to capture the moments on paper. I hope I was able to do justice to her vision.

I am an avid reader and have a BA degree with honors in English. I enjoy being a member of a couple of local book clubs. I enjoy vacationing with my family and friends and love entertaining and socializing. I simply love life.